MW01042272

FOSSENDOCKER BILL

GRAMPS AND THE NEW HOUSE

♥

A novel for the young and the young at heart

FOSSENDOCKER BILL
GRAMPS AND THE NEW HOUSE

Bill Dale Grizzle

The Fossendocker Bill Series
Book 1

Fossendocker Bill is a work of fiction. Names, characters, places, and incidents are the product of the author's imagination or used fictitiously. Any resemblance to actual persons, living or dead, business establishments, events, or locations is entirely coincidental.

Copyright © 2018 by Bill Dale Grizzle
All rights reserved. No part of this book may be reproduced, scanned, copied, distributed, or transmitted, in any print or electronic form, without permission from the author.
Short excerpts may be used for the purposes of reviews or book reports.

Cover photograph and design by Bill Dale Grizzle

Published by Bill Dale Grizzle

The Pine Log Press

An informal literary group dedicated to the production and distribution of quality, meaningful, and wholesome reading materials for children, young readers, and adults.

ISBN: 978-1-7294259-4-7

Published and printed in the United States of America

Thank you, Papa, for endowing me with a nickname like none other.
Thank you, Granddaddy, for showing me that anything is possible,
through faith and effort. Thank you both for your friendships, love, time,
and the wonderful examples you set before me.

This book is dedicated to the countless children who have encountered
circumstances similar to these described in this story. Young ones, and
teenagers alike, that have faced the challenges of moving to a new home,
entering new schools, making new friends, and yes, those who have been
bullied.
My thoughts and prayers are with you.

If you are, or have been, a victim of bullying, regardless of your age,
I strongly encourage you to tell someone.
Tell your parents, teachers, supervisors, law enforcement,
just tell someone.
Something can be done!

PROLOGUE

Harley and Pearl Bill, their three children, two dogs, a cat, and a talking bird had finally out grown their little house on the outskirts of Plainville. How this could have happened was not exactly clear. But there was one thing for certain, everything was about to change.

A few months ago, Mr. and Mrs. Bill began construction on a new house near the small community of Midway. This meant their oldest son, Ralph, would be going into the ninth grade at Cannonbay High School. Raelynn, the blond-haired, blue-eyed, apple of her parents eyes, would start the first grade at Midway Elementary. Their eleven-year-old son, Fossendocker, very much to his despair, would begin the sixth grade at Midway Middle School, instead of Plainville Middle where all his friends would be. Through very careful planning on the part of Mr. and Mrs. Bill, the house construction had been timed so that the family could move during the summer break from school, and that time was drawing closer and closer.

BILL DALE GRIZZLE

8

CHAPTER 1

"There's only two or three good things about the new house, Lenny." Fossendocker Bill explained to his best friend, Leonard Lee Duvall, as they peddled their bicycles around the quiet streets of Olde Towne, the subdivision where they both had lived all their lives. "It's really close to my grandparent's house."

"Well that's pretty cool, I guess," interrupted Leonard Lee, "it takes hours and hours to get to my grandparent's house."

Fossendocker paid little attention to the last comment his friend made. Right now it was not important how long it takes Lenny to get to his grandparent's house. First and foremost, in his mind, was the fact that he would soon be moving away. This horrible thought weighed heavily on his young mind. "And it's close to the creek and there's lots of woods to explore and play in. I sure hope you get to come see me sometime."

The pair rode on in silence for a while, both thinking about how different it was going to be not living within a few of hundred feet of your best friend.

"Hey Dock," Leonard finally broke the silence, "how's

your bicycle working since you got all that nasty grease off the gears and chain?"

"It works fine now," Fossendocker answered, then frowned to himself, remembering how mad his mother had been at him for getting grease on his new jeans, socks, and shoes. He choose not to share that with Leonard.

"How did you get all that nasty stuff off, anyway?" asked Leonard.

"Well, Lenny," Fossendocker replied as he rolled to a stop at the corner of their street. "I took it apart and put it in the dishwasher, the chain and the back wheel, anyway. I had to take that thing you put glasses and cups on out to get the wheel in." Then he calmly peddled away.

Leonard Lee Duvall was stunned at the solution his quick thinking friend had come up with and could only stare at him for several seconds. "Dock, you're the smartest guy I know," he called out. "How did you think of that?"

"Don't know, Lenny," Fossendocker shouted back over his shoulder, "it just popped into my head."

Leonard caught up with his friend already stopped in front of the Bill residence, but before he could question Fossendocker further about the dishwasher trick, he was sidetracked.

"Race you down to your house, Lenny. The last one there is a rotten egg." Fossendocker didn't even wave at his dad as he turned into the driveway, returning home from work. No time to wave, the race was on and he was not used to being a rotten egg. In this neighborhood there was no faster bicycle; he had taken everything off his bike that he could to reduce the weight. What was left was just barely enough to call a bicycle. But he didn't mind, he's Fossendocker Bill, the speed demon of Lamplighter Lane.

Without slowing down, Fossendocker whipped his bike onto the driveway at the Duvall house and slammed on the brake as hard as he could. This left a long black mark on the concrete.

Just as he turned to admire his tire mark, Leonard skidded to a halt beside him and turned to admire his own skid mark.

"Good one, Lenny," Fossendocker gave his buddy a high five. "that'll give your dad something to complain about."

"Yeah, he hates it when we do that, he says that it makes the place look tacky. You know who gets griped at, though, don't you?"

"Yeah," said Fossendocker, obviously not overly concerned about that. "Listen, Lenny, Gramps told me about a bike he saw on TV with two wheels in the back. Not like those big tricycle bikes that old people ride. The tires on this one were close together, like this." Fossendocker held his hands about eight inches apart. "Gramps said he'd help me build one if I can come up with the parts we need. Do you think you can get hold of some old bike parts? I think I know where I can get some stuff. You want in on the project, or not?"

"Sure I do," exclaimed Lenny.

"First of all," Fossendocker sounded serious, "we don't want anything but boy's bicycle parts. That means no girl's bicycle parts, okay."

Leonard nodded his commitment.

"Let's go to your room and get some paper and a pencil and I'll show you. Gramps says that we've got to have a plan. Fossendocker was already off his bicycle heading for the front door. Carelessly scrambling to catch up, Leonard almost tripped over his own bike, but all the while he was thinking that this is going to be good. Dock always came up with good stuff.

"Hey, Dock, how far is it to this new house of yours, anyway?" Leonard asked as he watched his best friend sketch out his big idea.

It was several seconds before Fossendocker acted like he'd even heard the question. Looking up he had a puzzled expression on his face, "I don't really know, Lenny."

"What do you mean, you don't know?" Leonard sounded as

puzzled as Fossendocker looked. "You've been there, haven't you?"

"Yeah I've been there........five or six times." What Leonard didn't realize was that his friend was trying to get the distance straight in his mind, "Dad always has to go by the lumber yard or the hardware store, or somewhere, so it's hard to tell how far it is. But I do know it's all the way over to Midway."

Leonard grunted, shook his head, and said, "*that's* a long way, Dock."

"Now look at this Lenny, how do you think this will work?" And just like that their focus was back on the drawing.

***

Harley Bill pulled into the drive and parked his pickup truck. While getting out he watched his eleven-year-old son and his best friend speeding down the street on their bikes. Shaking his head and with a slight smile, he quietly said. "Not a care in the world." He continued to watch the boys until they turned into the Duvall driveway, four houses down.

"Talking to yourself?" He turned to see Mrs. Bill standing on the front porch, her hands on her hips.

"To be a kid again." He stepped up onto the porch to greet his wife.

"Not that kid I hope," she snapped. "He's about to drive me up the wall."

"What has he done now?" Not really wanting to hear, but being the boy's father, he felt like he needed to ask.

Mrs. Bill told her husband about the new pair of jeans with grease all over the right leg. "Well at least he didn't get it on his bed," she said, "but it was on one sock and one shoe. He said he had to, 'grease up his bicycle.' What *are* you going to do with that boy of yours?"

"What do you mean, boy of *mine*?" Mr. Bill stopped short

of the front door. "He's half yours you know."

"Not today, he's not." She gave her husband a little shove to get him started toward the door again.

As the couple entered the house, Mrs. Bill made a request. "Before you go over to the new house, would you please do something for me?"

"Sure sweetheart." He answered, giving her a hug and a little kiss on the cheek. "Sorry you've had a rough day. What do you need?" Mr. Bill hoped that comforting her might distract her thoughts from their son, who had proven himself to be quiet a handful, lately.

"I would like for you to mow the back yard. The grass is getting so tall back there I'm afraid one of the dogs will get lost. Ralph didn't get to it Saturday before he left because of that thunderstorm, remember."

Ralph was spending a few days at his mother's brother's house. His youngest child, Thurson and Ralph are the same age and are more like brothers than cousins. They have played together on the same baseball team since they were eight years old, and have excelled in every sport they've participated in. At this stage of their lives it seemed that all they thought about was sports, but that was okay. Neither Ralph nor Thurson had caused their parents many problems at all, up to this point, at least.

"I can do that," replied Mr. Bill. "Will you fix something for me to eat before I go? I'll take Fossendocker with me, if you'll round him up, and let him work for that pair of jeans he ruined." With that, he headed for the basement and the lawnmower.

Mrs. Bill sat down at the kitchen table with a glass of ice water. It had been a quiet afternoon for the most part. Fossendocker had been outside most of the day. In fact, he spends most of his time outside, every day, only making quick trips through the kitchen for a drink or to grab something to eat. "If only I didn't have to worry about him destroying the neighborhood," she said under her breath. Then she smiled at her thoughts of little

Raelynn. She'd been asleep for well over an hour. Apparently the tea parties, cooking pretend cakes and pies, and playing house with her dolls had gotten the best of her.

Within a few minutes the sound of the lawnmower filled her ears. Well, she thought, that quiet time was good while it lasted. She picked up the phone to call the Duvall's.

"Hello Pearl, how are you today?"

"Hi Sadie," replied Mrs. Bill, "I'm fine, and yourself." The two ladies swapped gossip and small talk for a few minutes before Mrs. Bill asked her to send Fossendocker home. "Please tell him I'm heating up the left over chicken and rice for him and his dad. He doesn't know it yet, but he's going with Harley to the new house."

"Yummm," said Mrs. Duvall, "maybe I'll leave him here to fix dinner for my family and I'll come have the chicken and rice." They laughed and were about to hang up when there was a loud clanking noise from the back yard followed by an even louder crash as something struck the outside back wall of the house.

The lawnmower went silent just as the alarmed Mrs. Bill stepped out the back door, the cordless phone still in her hand.

"FOSSENDOCKER!" Mr. Bill bellowed at the top of his voice.

Mrs. Bill cringed. She'd heard that bellow before. It was the kind of bellow that would make a rodeo bull cower. It was the kind of bellow that said her little boy might be in serious trouble. Putting the phone back to her ear she said, "Harley hit something with the mower. I'd better go."

"I heard him yelling; call me later. Bye," said Mrs. Duvall and hung up.

"Are you alright, Harley? What in the world did you run over?" Mrs. Bill was hurrying across the yard, but stopped in her tracks, as her husband, still seated on the riding lawnmower, turned to face her. She knew what those little globs of brownish-grayish stuff were. Those little globs that seemed to be all over the

14

unfortunate Mr. Bill.

"That's *grease* Harley." She was shaking her head in disbelief. "How did you get grease all over you?" Mr. Bill pointed at the house, there were little globs of brownish-grayish stuff splattered on the wall between the master bedroom windows. Lying on the ground a couple of feet from the house were the mangled remains of a grease gun.

"I ran over it." He paused to wipe a gob of grease from his lip. "It hit the tree and splattered me, bounced back, and before I could get stopped, I ran over it again. It came out from under the mower like a missile. We're just lucky it didn't go through a window."

"Well Harley, I'm glad you're not hurt. That scared the life out of me. When you finish out here, take those cloths off in the basement and be careful not to get them against anything, they're filthy." With those instructions Mrs. Bill whirled and started back to the house.

"Okay, sweetheart, okay. But when that boy gets home send him out here with some cleaning rags and some kind of cleaner."

***

Fossendocker and Leonard both looked up as the bedroom door opened, "Mooomm," Leonard drew out the word so that it almost sounded like a cow mooing. "This is a secret meeting of the Lamplighter Legends." Leonard protested with an unwelcoming expression and motioned with his hand for his mom to leave.

"Never mind your secret meeting, young man. Dock, your mom called and asked that I send you home. Your dad ran over something with the lawnmower in the backyard. I heard him yelling." Mrs Duvall nodded and bit her lower lip. "My guess is that you are in big trouble."

The two boys looked at each other with eyes as big as silver dollars. No need to wonder what it could have been that Mr. Bill

15

ran over. No need to ask each other what could have been left in the yard. They both knew.

"Dock, your dad is going to rip your head off and put it on an ant hill." Leonard's solemn voice gave Fossendocker the creeps. "Man, I can't believe you left your dad's grease gun out in the yard." Leonard started laughing as he visualized Mr. Bill running over the grease gun. "I wonder what it looks like now?"

"It's not funny, Lenny! I guess I'd better go home now." Fossendocker was up and headed for the door. "Bye, Lenny's mom."

"Bye, Dock, good luck." Mrs. Duvall's attention then turned to her son who was still laughing out loud. "Leonard Lee," she was giving him the infamous laser-eye look, "did *you* have anything to do with this? I want the whole story."

***

Fossendocker was walking in the front door of his house in less than a minute. Sounds from the kitchen told him that Mom was getting dinner ready. Maybe I should act like nothing's going on, or maybe I should just go to my room. His contemplations, however, were abruptly interrupted by a shriek from his mother, followed by her screaming voice.

"What in the.....that boy! I'm going to wring his neck!"

Peeking around the corner, he could see his mom down on her knees looking inside the dishwasher. "To my room, and hide in the closet," he whispered to himself as he slipped into the hallway without his mom seeing him.

"What are you doing, Dock?" Blurted Raelynn, who was now wide awake and standing in the doorway of her room. What rotten luck, his little sister had caught him slipping down the hallway.

Fossendocker put his finger to his lips, but it was too late.

"Young man, you get in your room right now!" yelled his

16

mother from the kitchen. There was not one hint of kindness in her voice and this caused Fossendocker concern. "You have really done it this time, buster. We'll deal with you when your dad comes in!"

Mrs. Bill was sitting at the kitchen table with her head in her hands, as her husband was putting the mower in the basement. Shortly afterward she heard him coming up the stairs.

"Is your son home yet?" he asked as he headed to their bedroom for clean cloths.

"Today, *he's your son*. I told you that, already." She shot back at him. "Now, you need to come look at this."

He headed for a shower instead.

Feeling a little better now, wearing clean cloths, and the grease shampooed from his hair, Mr. Bill headed for the kitchen. Just as he entered, his wife flopped open the dishwasher door and made a hand gesture for him to look inside. Kneeling down, he could see water standing in the tub, an entanglement of dishes from breakfast, and the top rack, unsecured on one side, cocked sideways. Then his eyes focused on clumps of dishwasher soap and globs of brownish-grayish grease. Their eyes met and they both shook their heads in disbelief.

A few minutes later, Mr. and Mrs. Bill and Fossendocker were seated around the small round table in the kitchen. A cartoon movie was on TV, keeping Raelynn occupied for a while.

"Fossendocker, we're going to give you the opportunity to explain yourself." His dad seemed to be putting great effort into staying calm. "What were you doing with my grease gun in the backyard? Why did you leave it out there? Do you realize someone could have been hurt, or the thing could have gone through a window?"

He had not given Fossendocker time to answer any of his questions, when his mom chimed in. "Your new jeans are ruined, you know. And how in the world did you get that grease in the dishwasher?"

17

There was a short pause, just long enough for him to feel his parents staring a hole right through him. "You're going to clean up that mess, young man," his mom added, "and you'd better hope that the dishwasher isn't ruined, too."

Another pause, maybe if he just sat there he wouldn't have to say anything. "*Well*?" snapped his dad. "What do you have to say for yourself?" Still no time to answer. "As soon as we're done here, you're going outside and clean that mess off the house, right after you clean up the dishwasher!"

Fossendocker had seen his otherwise calm parents pretty upset before, but this time they were about to blow their tops. If I say anything, he thought, it had better be good. "I didn't mean to leave it in the yard. I just forgot, that's all," he babbled on with his excuses. "My wheel was squeaking, and I got too much grease on it, and I got it on my jeans, I knew I would be in trouble, so I took my bike apart and put the chain and the wheel in the dishwasher to clean them up."

This is good he thought, and took a breath. They're listening to me. What he didn't realize, was that his parents were flabbergasted beyond words that their little boy would even consider such a remedy for his situation. "I mean, I had to get that stuff off or I would mess up more pants and then I would get grounded, and I wouldn't get to play with my best friend, and then we would be moved off to the new house and I'd never see him again." He caught his breath and without thinking he blurted out, "*it's all the new house's fault,* if I didn't have to move all this wouldn't have happened." He quickly hung his head, so his parents couldn't see the, where did that come from, look on his face. I can't believe I said that, he thought, but that might just work. I'll blame the new house. "And Dad," he muttered without looking up, "you're gone over there to the new house every day; I never see you any more, and you're not here to show me how to do stuff. It's all the new houses fault!"

Mr. Bill took his gaze off the top of Fossendocker's head

and looked at his wife. Her hard stare was beginning to soften. Oh no, she's falling for this load of junk, he thought, I'd better act quick. "Okay buddy boy, we'll do something about that last part starting today. Apparently we need to spend more time together. As soon as you finish all your cleanup," his dad continued, "you are going with me to the new house. You're going to help me do some work around there. A little father and son time, you might say. And while we're at it, we're going to let you work for your new jeans you ruined, and for a new grease gun, and for the cleaning liquid it takes to clean up your mess. Don't look so surprised, young fellow, maybe this will help teach you to be a little more responsible."

The eleven-year-old boy wasn't surprised, he was shocked! He absolutely could not believe his ears. His dad was going to *make* him work. Fossendocker knew this was it. Judgment had been passed; there was no getting out of this one. Looking at one parent, and then the other, he humbly asked the only thing that he could ask. "How long do I have to work?"

"We'll pay you two dollars an hour," his dad said. That's fair enough, I made two dollars a day when I was your age and helped my Daddy around the house. A new grease gun is about twenty dollars."

"Those jeans were sixteen dollars at Coleman's and a bottle of good cleaner is about four dollars," added his mom.

"We can get four or five hours of work in between the time I get home from the tire store and dark," said his dad, "so you can figure it out."

"Oh, and that's not all," Mrs. Bill was not quiet finished yet, "you're grounded. You can't go to Leonard's, and he can't come here, for a week. Is that clear?"

"Yes ma'am, it's clear," the downhearted young fellow mumbled.

"Good," stated his dad, "we'll eat our dinner and then you'll get busy."

Two hours later the cleanup was completed, with little

thanks to his mom and dad. They'd offered much advice on how to do the cleaning but very little actual help. Instead, they went into great detail explaining to him how he didn't need their help to make the mess, so he shouldn't need their help in cleaning it up, either. Fossendocker wasn't sure how, but somehow, that made more sense to his parents than it did to him.

Finally Mr. Bill and Fossendocker left for the new house. After a quick stop at the lumber yard for some 2X4's, they made their way toward Midway. Mr. Bill went over a list of things that needed to be done over the next few days, starting with gathering up the scrap wood and placing it on the pile that would be burned at a later time.

At sundown Mr. Bill called it a day and they headed home. Driving along the highway toward Plainville Fossendocker's dad spoke in his usual kind voice. "You did a good job this evening, son, maybe you will learn something from all this." Glancing to his right he realized that his words had fallen on deaf ears, for the exhausted boy was sound asleep on the truck seat beside him.

***

Meanwhile back on Lamplighter Lane, Mrs. Bill's blood pressure had somewhat returned to normal. She'd fixed Raelynn's supper and put her in the bathtub. She avoided an onslaught of questions from the sweet little girl about what kind of trouble her big brother was in by acting silly and playing a game with a rubber ducky.

About seven-thirty, Mrs. Bill started a short animated movie on DVD for Raelynn to watch while she cleaned up the kitchen. Holding her breath, she turned on the dishwasher. "Thank goodness," she whispered to the appliance, "I was so afraid you would be clogged up." Much to her relief the machine seemed to be working fine. "Well, at least you should be well lubricated for the next people that live here."

20

Sitting in the kitchen floor staring at the dishwasher; listening to the low hum of its motor, the exhausted lady of the house recalled every detail of her day. He must have put his bike parts in the dishwasher during that hour or so I was in Raelynn's room reading to her. Unbelievable, she thought, then shook her head to clear her mind of what her son had done. She considered making a cup of hot tea, but decided to wait until she put Raelynn to bed. Yeah, she could take a long bubble bath and sip a cup of tea then. "Right now I think I'll call Sadie back," she said out loud as she pulled herself up. "She's going to love this one."

The phone at the Duvall home rang only once when Leonard's shout caused her to flinch. "That you Dock?"

"*No*, it is not," Mrs. Bill was very stern, but civil, "and it won't be for a while. Your partner in crime is on restriction for a week. That means he can't come to your house and you can't come to his house, either. And no slipping out to meet in the street on your bikes."

"But Dock's mom," Leonard protested, "that's like I get punished for something I didn't do."

"Sorry about your luck, Lenny, but I'm *sure* you've done something in the past to deserve it, and I'm also quiet certain you'll do something in the future. Now, may I please speak to your mother."

When Mrs. Duvall came to the phone there was almost a laugh in her voice as she said. "What did you say to Leonard? He looked shocked!"

Mrs. Bill, on the verge of tears, shared the whole story with her best friend. Somehow managing to find a certain degree of humor in the situation, both ladies were laughing by the end of the story.

"Lord, Pearl, my Leonard Lee is rambunctious, but he can't hold a candle to your Fossendocker."

"Yes, I know," Mrs. Bill sighed, "the boy is absolutely impossible. Honestly, Sadie, I don't know where he gets it."

Mrs. Duvall chuckled. "You know where he gets it. You just don't want to admit it. My daddy has been friends with your daddy all his life, and he says Dock acts just like your daddy did when he was that age....into everything, and not happy unless he is into everything." They both laughed, then said goodnight.

"Come let me tuck you into bed my little pumpkin pie," Mrs. Bill said to Raelynn as she sat down heavily on the couch and gathered her baby girl into her arms.

"Okay, Mommy," answered the sleepy girl, who rarely gave any trouble about going to bed. Tonight, though, she seemed a little hesitant. "Mommy, are you really going to wring Dock's neck? I heard you say that, Mommy."

The sincere concern in Raelynn's voice for her brother was more than she could take. Tears flowed from her eyes as she held her baby girl tightly, but at the same time she couldn't help but laugh. "No darling, I'm not going to wring Dock's neck. Dock's in plenty of trouble alright, but I'm sure he'll survive it. So don't you worry about that Dock, okay? Come on now, sweetie, let's get you to bed, Mommy loves you."

CHAPTER 2

Harley Bill had been a hard worker all his life. He started out small with a single tire dealership two blocks from downtown Plainville. Granted, this was only a fair location, but the work ethic that his own dad taught him years before had stuck with him. Over the course of sixteen years his business in the downtown location had thrived. Plus, he'd added two more locations within the boundaries of Collie County, both were just as successful as the original store. Although the Bill family would not be considered rich by any means, they were finally in the position to build their dream house. Thanks to a lot of help from family members, and the fact that Mr. Bill did a lot of the work himself, their new house would be fully paid for when completed. This was very important to him, being a firm believer in living debt free. He hoped that he could find ways of passing this along to his own children.

Mr. Bill pulled his pickup truck into the drive at four-thirty-five. Fossendocker was out the front door, off the porch, and in the truck before his dad could even get his seat belt off. "Raring to go there, huh, young man?"

"*Yes sir,*" chirped Fossendocker. All the while he stared straight ahead. This had been one miserable day. Picking up scrap wood was nothing compared to what his mother had put him through. Oh sure, he got to go outside for a couple of hours, but only in the back yard. Most of his day, however, was spent reading, practicing math problems, helping his mom fold the laundry, cleaning out the stinky old bird cage, and playing with Raelynn. A whole week of this. And guess what? Mom says she still has a whole list of things that need to be done. Fossendocker sulked while he wallowed in his thoughts. Yep, this had been the first of a weeks worth of miserable days.

"I don't know about you, but I'd like to at least have a sandwich or something before we go," said his dad as he climbed out of the truck.

"I'll stay right here," mumbled Fossendocker, still staring through the windshield.

"Suit yourself. Just don't mess with any buttons or knobs." Stopping in his tracks, he turned around and snatched the key from the ignition switch. No way am I going to leave that temptation, he thought.

Day two was about the same as day one, picking up scrap lumber and trash and carrying it to the burn pile. This was indeed a boring task, but according to Fossendocker's calculations he should be finished with this job today.

The only obstacle in his way was the fact that his dad had instructed him to carry everything through the house and out the garage door. This made his trips twice as long as they would be if he could go out the back door, however, the back porch and steps were not yet complete. A homemade ramp, about a foot wide, was how the workers had been coming and going from the house. His dad had explained to him how dangerous the ramp was and that he didn't want him to fall off into the ditch that ran along beside the foundation. The ditch that had not yet been filled in with dirt. Still, this shortcut would make things so much easier, and faster.

In spite of his dad's stern warning to stay off the makeshift ramp, Fossendocker's mind traipsed down that path of mischief. The *path* that had led him to trouble so many times. While Dad is back in the bedrooms working on closet shelves I'll make a few trips out the back door and save some time, he thought. I'll make sure I get finished with this junk so I can help Dad with the work benches in the basement tomorrow. I'll be careful, and it'll be okay. His mind was working overtime. Using the ramp might even be fun. It will be kind of like walking the gang plank on a pirate ship.

However, sometimes even the best of plans, made by the wisest of men, go terribly wrong. As Fossendocker was making his third return trip up the ramp he was in a sword fight with the evil Captain Crank, the most fearsome of all pirates. He intended to defeat this evil pirate, take control of his ship and his treasure chest, and free the captives held in the belly of this vessel. It was a fight to the end on the gang plank over shark infested waters.

Fossendocker's dad came running as fast as he could when he heard his son's cries for help. "Where are you, son?" Mr. Bill called out, running around each room, into the garage, and finally into the back yard. "What's wrong? Where are you?"

"Down here," Fossendocker shouted, sputtering as he did so, "in the ditch."

Mr. Bill could not believe his eyes as he rushed over to the ramp. There was his son wedged between the concrete foundation of the new house and the dirt side of the ditch, upside down. "Are you hurt?" his dad asked, getting down onto the ground so he could catch hold of his ankles. "Are you okay?"

"I don't know, Dad," muttered Fossendocker, "I'm stuck."

Observing the boy's flailing arms and kicking legs, Mr. Bill made an assumption that there was no terrible damage done. He got a firm grip on the boy's ankles and with one quick motion pulled him from the ditch and sat him down on the ramp. A quick check revealed no broken bones, only a scrape on his forehead and his nose, and a little dirt in his mouth.

"Where are your glasses, buddy?" asked his dad. Between the spitting and sputtering trying to get the dirt out of his mouth, he managed to point down into the ditch. His dad fished them out and held them in front of Fossendocker's face, he could see that they were broken. Beyond the broken glasses, Fossendocker focused in on his very unhappy-looking dad.

"This house is trying to kill me, Dad!"

"Don't talk to me right now," was his dad's stern reply to that claim, as he half dragged the boy to his truck and his first aid-kit.

"Is that going to burn?" The boy pulled back in protest of the dreaded medicine.

"No!" snapped his dad as he liberally applied an antibiotic ointment to his scrapes.

Having tended to all of Fossendocker's scrapes, Mr. Bill then grabbed a roll of electrical tape from his tool box and mended the broken glasses as best he could. "That will have to do for now," he said handing the patched glasses to his son. Then he got really close to the boy's face and said in a calm but stern voice. "I'm glad you're not hurt, son, but if you get back on that ramp again you're going to be in so much trouble it will make your head spin. Do I make myself clear?"

Still pretty shook up from the incident, the boy nodded and muttered, "I'm sorry, Daddy. I was just trying to go faster so I can help you tomorrow when you build the work benches in the basement."

"Right now you just need to worry about the task at hand," said his dad, as he sat down on the tailgate of his truck. He sat there for some time, silently staring at the ground between his feet. Fossendocker didn't realize that his daddy was so relived that his son wasn't injured, and he was also so preoccupied with thanking God for that favor, that he had not yet considered the fact that Fossendocker had not followed instructions. Even worse yet, he

26

had disobeyed his dad. But as it always is with dad's and mom's, they quickly come to their parental senses, and the boy would realize that soon enough.

"Well, it appears that you're okay," Mr. Bill finally said, "so get back to your job. The painters are supposed to be here tomorrow, so we need to have everything cleaned up for them. *And stay off that ramp*." His dad was shaking his finger at him, so Fossendocker stuck to nodding his head. "We will talk about this some more on the way home." With that they were both back to work.

Within a couple of hours all the scrap wood, drywall, and trash had been removed from the house. Mr. Bill had finished his project, and between the two of them they had swept and vacuumed all the floors.

"We're ready for the painters, buddy boy. We're really getting close to finishing now." The excitement in his dad's voice made the boy's head spin. "We'll be finished and ready to move in before you know it."

Along with his spinning head, now Fossendocker's heart sank a little. He didn't want to move out here in the middle of nowhere and go to a new school where he didn't know anyone. No more nice quiet level streets where he could ride his bike. The whole thing really stinks, he thought. Maybe I'll go live with Lenny. Those thoughts were short-lived, though. Still, his young mind couldn't understand how his dad could be so excited about moving to this place.

"Let's go home. I'll bet you're hungry, aren't you?" Mr. Bill playfully rubbed the top of his boy's head.

At least Dad doesn't seem too mad about me falling in the ditch, thought Fossendocker, as he climbed into the truck.

A few minutes into the ride home, Mr. Bill spoke up. "Your mother is going to have a cow about your glasses, you know. That's two pair since Christmas, isn't it?" Fossendocker felt like this was the sort of question that really didn't need to be answered, so he kept his mouth shut. "You're a smart boy, Dock, you know that, and I know that you have an active imagination. You enjoy working on your bike and things, and you like to build stuff, and sometimes you break things with that curiosity of yours. But you need to listen to your mother and me. I promise there would be a lot less trouble in your life if you did." Fossendocker still said nothing, he just looked out the window. "I mean, like the grease gun thing, what in the world ever possessed you to have that thing outside, anyway?"

The boy couldn't let this opportunity slip by. Since his parents had bombarded him with so many questions the day before, and hadn't really given him a chance to say anything, he had to respond to this. "Well, Gramps always says that the squeaky wheel gets the grease. My bike wheel was squeaking."

Instantly a very recent conversation with his father-in-law popped into Mr. Bill's head. They were talking about the county government and how much a certain group of people constantly complained about things, yet it seemed like that group of people always got what they wanted. Although his son was sitting only a few feet away during this conversation, Mr. Bill had no idea that the boy was paying any attention to them.

The eleven-year-old always hung on every word that his Gramps said, so why did he not notice that the boy lit up like a light bulb, when the older gentleman declared. 'Well, you know what I always say, the squeaky wheel gets the grease.' Remembering the look on his son's face, Mr. Bill shook his head and softly said, "a seed was planted."

"What seed, Dad?"

"Oh, nothing son," he replied, reaching over to rub the boy's fuzzy, almost white hair again. "Let's go wash that dirt out of your hair."

They drove on toward Plainville, the setting sun sent rays of different shades of red and orange across the sky behind them. "Red sky at night is a sailor's delight," Mr. Bill said while looking into the rear-view mirror.

"What does that mean, Dad?" Fossendocker asked as he twisted around so he could also see behind them.

"I've never asked a sailor," he replied, "but to me it means that I can rest easy tonight because the storm has passed."

This satisfied the boy although he had no idea his dad was really saying that he was no longer upset with his son for falling into the ditch. *But* the part about being disobeyed *would* be dealt with later.

***

Early the next morning the Bill's were up and around the breakfast table planning their day. "I talked to Sadie last night, and she said that we could leave Raelynn with them." Leonard Lee's sixteen year old sister, Rhonda, adored Raelynn, and the feeling was mutual. She could keep the young one occupied, and vice-versa. Mrs. Bill continued with her plan, "Fossendocker and I will go to the optical center at Mega-Mart for his new glasses. His prescription is still current so they should be able to have them ready in two or three hours. In the mean time we—"

Mr. Bill held up his hand to interrupt. "Do us a favor and get him some glasses that are more durable than the last few pair, okay. On second thought, just get a pair of lenses and I'll have Mr. Clarence at the welding shop fabricate some frames out of some of that old scrap steel he has lying around. They should be durable enough."

Both adults got a laugh out of this. Fossendocker, however, failed to see the humor in it. In a split second his mind had constructed a vision, and it was not a pretty vision. He could just see himself with a pair of homemade glasses, as big as a car bumper, all rusty and ugly. Everybody would laugh at him. How in the world could he ride his bike, or climb trees, or for that matter, do anything, in those ridiculous things. The look of concern on his face made his parents laugh even louder.

"You see how the boy's mind works," said his dad. "He could just see himself in a pair of homemade, steel glasses." They laughed some more, then finally got the conversation back on track.

Mrs. Bill continued, "I'll pick up the rest of the ceiling fans and the light fixtures."

"Don't forget to pick out the lights for the front and back porches," interjected her husband.

"I've already got those picked out. I know exactly what I want," she answered. "And while we're there I want to look at dishwashers."

"The painters are going to start today. They'll be there for about five days, they said. The ceramic tile guys are scheduled for next Wednesday." Mr. Bill took a deep breath, "things are moving along very well. We shouldn't have any problem moving in before school starts back."

Don't they ever get tired of talking about that new house, Fossendocker thought. He rolled his eyes at the glass of milk he was finishing. I know I sure get tired of hearing about it.

"Take your sister with you, and both of you brush your teeth, please, top and bottom teeth," his mother instructed. "We'll leave as your dad leaves for work."

As they pulled into the Duvall's driveway, Fossendocker formulated a plan. Mom and Lenny's mom will talk for an hour, so Lenny and I can hit the trampoline for a while.

"*Stay* in the car," his mom said with the tone she uses when she really means what she's saying. "I'll only be a minute."

Fossendocker was dwelling on how his parents are all the time messing up his plans, when he saw Leonard's figure appear at the front door. Hey, this might work out yet, he thought. As Lenny opened the storm door, though, a hand came from nowhere, grabbed him by the arm and quickly pulled him back into the house. Wow, thought Fossendocker, that was just like a movie on

30

TV. Just as someone is about to escape from the bad guys, they get caught from behind. The next figure to appear in the doorway was his mother.

"By the time we get to Mega-Mart the optical center should be open," said Mrs. Bill. "But if they aren't, we can look for some new shoes for you to wear to church. And remember we have that wedding to go to in a couple of weeks. You'll need them for that anyway."

"Yuck, yuck, and double yuck, Mom! Really, a wedding?" Fossendocker cringed at the thought of having to get dressed up for something that wasn't church. "Who wants to go to a wedding? That's boring, Mom."

"Maybe so," answered his mom, "but Matt Stamps started working for your dad when he was sixteen years old and has been a loyal employee for sixteen years now. He's almost like part of your dad's family, and I wouldn't want to think how hard it would have been on your dad building the new house without Matt's help at the stores. So, you're going, and that's that."

As they turned into the Mega-Mart parking lot it started to rain. "I didn't know it was going to rain today," said Mrs. Bill. Thankfully, she was lucky enough to find a parking space close to the entrance, which she took full advantage of rather than dealing with an umbrella. "Watch for cars," she instructed her son, and they quickly headed for the entrance doors.

Once inside they discovered that the optical center would not be open for another half hour so they had time to do their shoe shopping, and even time to pick out a new dress shirt and tie for Mr. Bill to wear to the wedding.

"Come on, Mom," said Fossendocker, getting a little anxious. "They're open now. I look like a real dork in these glasses with tape all over them."

"Okay, okay," said his mom, "let's go." Pearl Bill hated being rushed, and for that very reason her middle child was her least favorite shopping companion.

"Here are the most popular frames for young people," said the lady in the optical center. "We have quiet a selection, as you can see. Do you want the same frames or something similar to what you have now?"

Mrs. Bill was explaining to the lady that something more durable would be in order when Fossendocker exclaimed. "These are the ones I want!" His mom and the lady turned to see that he had on a pair of thick black plastic frames.

"I don't think so," his mom was shaking her head. "Those are what your Gramps wore when he was in high school."

"Why did I say that?" Mrs. Bill whispered to the saleslady, who looked puzzled at the question. "Knowing that his grandfather had glasses like that will only make him want them even more." She shrugged her shoulders.

"Maybe that didn't register," suggested the sales lady.

"Fat chance," whispered Mrs. Bill.

The two ladies continued to look at the more fashionable metal frames. "They are durable," whispered the saleslady, "and they are only twenty-one dollars." Mrs. Bill glanced back at her son. He was still wearing the black frames, standing in front of the mirror. She could almost read the boys thoughts. If my Gramps had glasses like these, then I've got to have some, too.

"I don't want him to look like a geek," his mom whispered back to the lady. "But he is the one who has to wear them."

The sales lady agreed. "You're absolutely right, ma'am, and besides, I think he's kind of cute."

"So, Fossendocker, those are the ones you want?" The boy jumped straight up while turning a half circle in mid-air. The big smile on his face answered that question. "Well, alright, but I don't know what your dad is going to think about your choice."

"By the way," said the saleslady. "We have a special sale on now, purchase one pair and the second pair is half price. Never hurts to have a spare pair. Two of my three sons wore glasses from about the same age as your son. I know how deadly they can be on

32

eye-wear, but they eventually grow out of the three-pair-a-year stage."

Mrs. Bill graciously thanked the saleslady for her recommendations and kind words. With the fitting and the sales transaction completed, the saleslady, in turn, thanked Mrs. Bill and Fossendocker for their business. She then told him that since his prescription was not complex the lab could make them right there; his glasses would be ready in about three hours.

Leaving the store his mom dropped a five dollar bill into a plastic pail. An elderly gentleman wearing a tall, funny-looking hat cheerfully thanked her and gave him a lollipop. Fossendocker kept looking back at the man as they headed for the car. "Who is that man, Mom, and what's he doing?"

"Those men do a lot of charity work for the children's hospital." Getting into the car she added, "ask Gramps, he knows about stuff like that."

During the ten minute drive to the home supply warehouse, Fossendocker didn't say a word. His mind was full of thoughts ranging from the man with the funny hat to how sick he was of this restriction business. He'd had a little time to think about the situation, and somehow he just could not make the crime fit the punishment. I mean I've done other stuff that didn't work out like it was supposed to, he was thinking, like when things end up broken or Dad's tools get lost. They've never made me pay for stuff before. That stupid grease gun must have been really important to Dad.

"Penny for your thoughts," said his mom as she pulled into a parking space. "Why so quiet today?"

"Do I have to go with Dad to the new house today?" Giving his mom the best sad-puppy eyes he could, "I'd like to show Lenny my new glasses."

"Yes, you're going with your dad. And no, you are not going to Lenny's. He can see your new glasses soon enough. Now, come help me pick out a ceiling fan for your new bedroom."

Finally, after what seemed like hours and hours of looking at hundreds and hundreds of light fixtures, ceiling fans, dishwashers, window blinds, and curtain rods, they had the back of the SUV packed, and the back seat loaded down.

"Do you think they have my glasses ready yet, Mom?" Fossendocker asked as he fastened his seat belt.

Mrs. Bill glanced at her watch before starting the car. "No, buddy, not yet. Let's stop at Miss Millie's for some lunch before we go back to Mega-Mart, okay?"

"Sure," piped Fossendocker. Miss Millie was the sweet old lady that had operated a tiny cafe on Franklin Avenue across from the County Courthouse for almost fifty years. Legend has it that when Miss Millie opened this little cafe, with only one thing on the menu, she stated that she would, 'give it fifty years; if I don't make it by then I'll shut the doors.' Now that it's getting close to fifty years, the locals are wondering if she will stay open. The only thing that Miss Millie will say about it is, 'you'll have to come by on the twenty-eighth day of July and see.'

Scores and scores of people of all ages, from all around the area, had secretly been planning a big celebration to thank Miss Millie for her years of faithful service to the community. It was a known fact that she had given much of herself over the years. Whether it be one of the churches, a social organization, a charity, the hospital, or a family in need. Somehow Miss Millie always knew of the need, and was there to assist in whatever way she could. Although most of her kind deeds were done in secret, or at least that's what she thought, nothing was ever expected from those who knew of her assistance. She was quick to remind them, however, to help someone else sometime in their lifetime.

Once inside the little cafe, Mrs. Bill and Fossendocker seated themselves at the only available table. There were seven other tables arranged around a horseshoe-shaped counter, where customers sat on stools to enjoy their lunch. No two tables matched, and not many of the stools and chairs were alike. One table, exclusively for kids, was from the old library and was too short for anyone but kids.

The little lady with short, silver hair and sparkling blue eyes, approached their table. Reaching out, she gave Fossendocker a frisky rub on the head. Winking a hello to Mrs. Bill she spoke to the boy as she inspected the wounds on his nose and forehead. "Good thing you're thick skinned," she cheerfully declared as she gathered his limp frame into her arms, giving his a huge hug. "There could have been something broken besides your specs."

Obviously she had already heard about his little accident, most likely from his dad.

How can such a small lady squeeze so hard, he wondered, as he escaped from her grasp and settled back into a sitting position.

"We sure are going to miss you at Plainville when you all get moved over to Midway. That school just won't be the same without you, Dock." Winking at Mrs. Bill once more, "Dock, you want crust or no crust this time?"

"No crust, and a glass of milk." Almost feeling the glare from his mother he quickly added, "please."

"And for you, Pearl, chicken salad salad and iced tea?"

"Miss Millie, I'm still amazed how you always know what people want to eat," Mrs. Bill jokingly said as she caught hold of the older lady's hand and gave it a squeeze.

"ESP my dear, ESP." Returning the hand squeeze, she was off to get their food and check on the other customers.

"Mom, why doesn't Miss Millie sell hamburgers and hot dogs and french fries like everybody else?" Fossendocker had often wondered about that, but this was the first time he'd ever asked.

Mrs. Bill took a deep breath. "Because Miss Millie is not like everybody else. She started her business making chicken salad sandwiches, and that's what she stuck with. Everything is homemade. She cooks her chicken for the chicken salad right here.

She even bakes her own bread. Everything she serves here is either grown in her garden or by someone here in Collie County, at least while it's in season. Peanut butter is the only exception, but it's what she does with the peanut butter that makes it so special. I can still remember those sandwiches and glasses of ice-cold milk from my own childhood."

"What does she do to it, Mom? I know it's a lot better than the peanut butter we have at home."

His mom continued her story. "We're not exactly sure, but we think she mixes honey and a little bit of apple sauce into the peanut butter. It makes it a little sweet and creamy."

Miss Millie had added her peanut butter sandwiches, which she called 'peanut better,' to the menu about five years after opening the cafe. Folks claim she'd said, 'some children don't want a chicken salad sandwich; why some of them don't even like chicken salad, but they gotta eat, too.' Someone, back around 1965 or '66, much to the delight of the local children, painted a sign on a piece of plywood that proclaimed that very statement. It hung outside on the side of the little cafe for twenty or twenty-five years, until it finally decayed and fell to the ground.

Miss Millie brought their food. A big, thick peanut better sandwich, the crust neatly trimmed from the edges, for Fossendocker. And for his mom, a generous helping of chicken salad sitting in a bed of fresh lettuce, surrounded by homegrown tomato wedges. Fossendocker hardly noticed the basket of crackers and the mason jar of homemade salad dressing. His attention was on his peanut better sandwich. He took a big bite, and before he knew it, his sandwich was gone.

"Yum," he said. "That was *soooo* good!" While his mom finished her lunch, he occupied his time looking at the dozens of old photographs that covered the interior walls of the cafe, occasionally taking a sip of his milk. Most of them were black and white prints in inexpensive frames. He'd heard that from time to time some famous person would stop by for Miss Millie's world famous chicken salad, but he had never seen anyone famous eating here. Well, maybe you could count the mayor, and one time there was this old guy that used to play professional baseball. But as far as Fossendocker was concerned, that was about it.

Mrs. Bill finished her lunch and paid the check. She said her goodbyes to Miss Millie, said hellos to a pair of ladies coming in, and was finally on the way to the car for their return trip to the Mega-Mart.

An hour later Fossendocker proudly sat in the front seat of his mother's SUV sporting a brand new pair of glasses. And not just any glasses, these were glasses like his Gramps used to wear. Yep, thought Fossendocker, this is a special day, and this is my new look.

"One more stop before we head home," said his mom, "I need to pick up a few things at the grocery store. Sunday is Grams' birthday, you know, and we're having a birthday dinner for her at their house."

"Is everybody going to be there?" Fossendocker asked.

"Yes, they are, and Ralph will be coming home."

The boy frowned and made a disapproving, growling sound.

"Well, I miss him, whether you do or not." Her words were kind of sharp, so the boy elected to keep quiet for the remainder of the trip.

Back at their home on Lamplighter Lane, Fossendocker helped his mom take the groceries into the house. The skies had cleared and it had turned out to be a beautiful day.

"I think I'll walk down to the Duvall's to get Raelynn," said Mrs. Bill. "It's such a pretty day, the walk will be good for me."

"I'll go get her!" exclaimed Fossendocker as he headed for the front door.

"Oh no you don't," snapped his mom. "You get back in here. I've got something for you to do. You have had that bedroom all to yourself for almost a week and it's upside down."

Fossendocker slumped into the nearest chair, "*Mmooom,*" he sighed. The boy knew what was coming next.

"This was not a day off. That room needs to be cleaned up and the sooner you get to it, the sooner you'll be done." Mrs. Bill was on the front porch when she added, "I'll be back in ten minutes, and I want to see some progress."

Several minutes later Fossendocker dragged himself from the chair and down the hallway to his and Ralph's bedroom. Mom was right, it was up-side down. There were toys, games, and books all over the place. His dresser drawers were standing open with clothes hanging out. The jeans and tee-shirt he'd had on yesterday when he toppled head first into that ditch were thrown into the corner by the closet. The desk that he shared with is big brother was completely littered with drawing paper and pencils. What a mess, he thought, as he started tossing his toys into the toy chest, I sure am going to miss my room when we move. Sadness clouded his young mind as thoughts of leaving this home for another raced through his head. He wouldn't even be sharing a room with Ralph.

He wouldn't be sharing a room with Ralph. The thought seemed to be stuck in his head. Suddenly joy chased away the sadness he was feeling and he said out loud, "I won't have to share a room with Ralph!" Jumping onto the bed, he started bouncing up and down. Big brothers are a pain in the backside, anyway, he was thinking, always bossing you around and stuff. No more of that junk; he makes me so mad sometimes. Again he yelled, "I won't have to share a room with Ralph!" This bounce took him almost to the ceiling.

"You'd better not be jumping on the bed," his mother's voice boomed down the hallway, and her tone told him that she meant business. Jumping on the bed was not allowed in the Bill home. They had a trampoline for that sort of activity.

Fossendocker was safely back on the floor gathering his dirty cloths for the hamper when his mom and Raelynn appeared in the door way. She gave him that, I know you were jumping on the bed look, so he moved faster to distract her. Cramming things back into the dresser drawers, he slammed them shut.

"Okay," his mom said, "okay, I see what you're doing."

Somehow he knew this was not approval of his cleaning skills. But he stuck with it, ending up under the bed dragging out comic books, Ralph's sports magazines, assorted other papers, and a couple pair of socks.

"Dock, let me see your new glasses." He loved to hear Raelynn's sweet little voice, and he loved to hear her laugh. He was pleased that his little sister was interested in his new glasses.

Pulling himself to a sitting position on the floor, Raelynn stood before him studying his face. "Yep, Mommy," she finally said in a definite and knowledgeable tone. "He looks like a Greek."

Mrs. Bill felt her face flush as she watched Fossendocker's smile fade from his. How in the world did she hear me whisper to Sadie that his new glasses made him look like a 'geek?' She bit her lower lip. Think fast, Pearl, she thought. I know that boy's not going to take that sitting down.

"What does she mean, I look like a Greek? What's that supposed to mean?" His voice was just on the verge of sounding frantic.

His mom was searching for a reply. "You know, a Greek is someone from the country of Greece." With that she turned and headed for the kitchen, hoping to avoid any farther questions. "How about spaghetti for dinner tonight? Dad will be home early and he'll be ready to eat."

Raelynn was still standing in front of her brother looking as if she was trying to decide if she liked Fossendocker's new look. Finally, she lunged at him, threw her arms around his neck and whispered, "I like your new glasses, Dock."

Her brother managed a word of thanks as he returned the hug but he was pretty much distracted. He was still trying to figure out the Greek thing.

Raelynn darted out leaving him sitting in the floor, and

within a few seconds he could hear her in her room talking to her dolls. Back at it, he thought, and started sorting the things that were under the bed a few minutes before. He made a neat stack of his comic books and placed them on the shelf over the desk, and then turned his attention to Ralph's magazines. In the process of stacking them on the shelf, he noticed a folded piece of paper sticking out of one. Thinking that it was probably some left over schoolwork, in one quick motion he pulled the paper out, unfolded it, and gave it a speedy glance.

Ralph's junk, he thought, then read aloud, "'Dear Becky,'" but then he stopped. His eyes were about to pop out of his head; he could not believe what he was reading. A love-letter to a girl! Looking quickly to the bottom of the page he almost lost it. There was a big heart with an arrow through it. Right smack dab in the middle of the heart were the words, 'Ralph loves Becky.' Then there was a bunch of X's and O's. He knew these meant kisses and hugs, because that's what Grams always put on his birthday cards.

Struggling to maintain his composure, he refolded the letter and stuck it inside one of his comic books. I'll finish reading that later, he thought, I might get caught with it now. *This* is going to be some good ammo to use on that Ralph. Still fighting back laughter, he finished his chore and called his mom for an inspection.

"It will do for now," said his mom. "Now wash up for supper. Dad's on his way home, and he wants to be on the way to the new house as soon as he can. Gramps is going to come over and help you two today." His mom started back to the kitchen to finish dinner. "By the way, Leonard Lee said hello."

Gramps was all he needed to hear, and he quickly said, "I'm ready to go." His thoughts were not on Leonard Lee, or the love-letter, or his restriction, he was only thinking of seeing Gramps, and showing off his new glasses.

Fossendocker had been at the dinner table for ten minutes when he heard his dad come in the front door. Raelynn rushed to meet her daddy.

40

"How's my little sweetheart?" He asked as he swept her up into his arms and walked toward the kitchen.

"I'm fine Daddy. I had fun at Rhonda's house. Did you sell a tire today, Daddy?"

Touched by her concern for his day, he held her tight and said. "Yes, I did, thank you for asking."

Mrs. Bill caught her husband's eye as soon as he entered the kitchen, gave him a subtle zip your lip sign, then cut her eyes toward Fossendocker, who was seated in his customary chair. His son was looking toward him sporting his new glasses; his new, big, black-plastic-framed, glasses. And he was wearing a very pleased grin on his face.

Fossendocker had just recently figured out that his parents could communicate without actually saying anything. He had not yet cracked the code, so he didn't know exactly what they were saying, but they were for certain saying something. And he figured it was probably about him.

Mr. Bill looked back at his wife with the, 'what were you thinking,' look.

Mrs. Bill returned her husbands glare with the, 'I don't know what I was thinking. I let him pick them out,' look.

The table was set. Mr. and Mrs. Bill and Raelynn took their places at the table, and Mr. Bill spoke a few words of thanks for the meal.

"How do you like my new glasses, Dad?" Fossendocker finally blurted out. "Mom says that Gramps had some like these a long time ago."

"As long as you're happy with them," his mother quickly said, before his dad could respond. "After all, you are the one that has to wear them. Isn't that right, Daddy?"

Mr. Bill was caught off guard. Now he certainly couldn't say what he was going to say. So he just stared at his wife, and she stared right back.

"I like Dock's new glasses," declared Raelynn, without a

clue that a tense moment evaporated when they all looked at her spaghetti sauce covered face.

The Bill family continued their meal, sharing small talk. Fossendocker told his dad about having lunch at Miss Millie's Cafe, and his mom explained which light and which fan went in which room. Somehow, Mr. Bill avoided having to comment on Fossendocker's new glasses at all. For this he was thankful.

CHAPTER 3

"Please be careful with the light fixtures," Mr. Bill said to his son. "Remember there are glass parts in those boxes." He was in a hurry to get to the new house for more than one reason, so he was trusting Fossendocker to help transfer the light fixtures and ceiling fans from the family car to his pickup truck.

"You know Gramps is going to meet us there today, and we need to get there to check on the painters. Just in case they need anything besides the color list that your mother has been working on for a month."

"Mom let me pick the color for my bedroom that I wanted," said Fossendocker. Then he added with reserved excitement, "well, sort of."

"What do you mean by, 'sort of?'" His dad asked, knowing already that his choices had been limited.

"Well, she showed me three colors and asked me which one I liked best."

"Well, son, which one did you pick?" His dad continued the conversation, hearing the enthusiasm in his son's voice. He knew this move was going to be hard on his youngest boy, leaving his neighborhood where he was so well liked and popular with the other kids, and most of all leaving Leonard Lee Duvall. Fossendocker was born nine days before Leonard and, since their mothers were best friends, the boys were like brothers.

"I wanted blue, but I had to pick a kind of chocolate milk color because Mom said it would go good with my fabrics.....what ever fabrics are."

"Good choice, buddy boy, I'm sure you'll be happy with it. Now let's ride. We don't want to make Gramps wait too long, because he might go on the warpath."

This got a laugh from the boy. Grams often joked with their grandchildren about the Native American heritage of their grandfather. When they weren't seeing eye to eye she would say, "Gramps is on the warpath," and other silly stuff like that. Fossendocker's thoughts took a journey through some of the stories that Gramps had told him, as he and his dad made their way toward Midway. The boy loved those stories, and he could listen to them over and over. He could hardly wait until Sunday when he would ask Gramps to tell them one. After all, it had been quiet a while since he'd heard a good story.

Westward out highway 57 they went with their load of lights and fans. Much to the delight of Harley Bill, the summer months had not brought the same relentless heat as the year before. The boy cut his eyes toward his dad as he heard him quietly thank God for the mild weather. "It sure makes it easier to work long hours when the heat isn't sapping your energy. Don't you think so, Dock?" His dad reached out to give him a pinch on the arm, which was quickly avoided with a giggle.

They backed up to the downstairs garage door, and the pair carefully unloaded the truck. They stored the ceiling fans and light fixtures in the concrete reinforced room that would later serve as their severe weather shelter. Mr. Bill had installed a heavy steel door very early in the building project to store his tools and other stuff that he didn't want, 'walking off the job site.' Fossendocker had thought that was a funny way to put it, but he knew exactly what his dad meant. "They'll be safe in there until we're ready to install them," he'd just said when they heard the familiar voice belonging to Gramps.

"You two down there taking a nap?" He yelled down the stairway, then made his way down to the basement.

"*Gramps*," shouted Fossendocker and raced to the stairs to meet his grandfather.

Gramps knelt down, taking the boy into his wide open arms, and gave him a big bear hug. "How ya been, Dock? I haven't seen you in such a long time I almost forgot what you look like. Let me take a look at that mug of yours. Yep, a little skinned up but I do believe you'll survive." Then he squeezed his grandson again for good measure.

Hardly able to breathe, much less talk, the boy managed to mumble. "You saw me the other day, Gramps, remember?"

"That's right I did. Well, it seems like a long time." Gramps loosened his hold on the boy and allowed him to wiggle free.

"Gramps, see my new glasses. Mom says that you had some just like mine a long time ago when you were in high school."

"I sure did. I reckon all the boys wore that kind of glasses. We didn't have all those fancy glasses like they have now, back in those days." He stood up and started toward his son-in-law with his big, strong hand extended. "Harley, good to see you, son." Gramps always wanted to shake hands. It didn't matter if he had seen you yesterday. Today is not yesterday, and today we shake hands. That was his belief.

Mr. Bill had great a respect for his father-in-law. In fact he was almost like a father to him. Twelve years earlier his own parents had relocated to a year-round warmer climate. 'Better for their aching joints,' they claimed. So visits once or twice a year were normal now. In the absence of his own father, his relationship with Gramps had grown stronger and stronger.

Born, Joseph William Whitefox, Gramps was a member of the Seminole Indian Tribe. His father had left south Florida as a young man to work for the railroad. By chance, he was working on a stretch of tracks near Jefferson University where he met a young lady in a restaurant one night. This young lady, whom was of Creek and French decent, captured his heart, and after she completed her college education, they married and settled in Collie County. Anna Mae, their first born, was followed three years later by Joseph.

Without a doubt, Gramps was the most patriotic American Mr. Bill had ever had the pleasure of knowing. A Vietnam Veteran, he was awarded a Silver Star, a Bronze Star, and two Purple Hearts for bravery and injuries sustained in combat. The flag of the United States of America flies at his house every day, and he never fails to pay respects to his fellow servicemen on Memorial Day and Veterans Day. Mr. Bill had often wondered how Gramps could have such a great love for his country, considering how his country had treated his ancestors. Someday, when the time was right, he would ask him about that.

"What's the plan, Harley?" Gramps asked. "We're going to build some work benches, right?"

"We sure are, Gramps," spoke up Fossendocker. His dad smiled and pulled a folded piece of paper from his shirt pocket.

"See what you think of this, Gramps," said Mr. Bill, unfolding the paper to reveal drawings of his basement workshop. "Work benches along this wall and this wall, with shelves along this wall. A cabinet here would be convenient for small power tools, hammers, clamps, and things like that."

"Looks good to me. What do you think, Dock?" Gramps gave his grandson a wink. "Just tell me what to do first."

A few hours later the three stood in the middle of the work shop space looking around. "Another productive day like today and this will be ready for me to move in all my tools," said Mr.

Bill. "Can you make it tomorrow evening, Gramps?"

"I sure can," answered Gramps, "It looks to me like you'll be ready to install lights and ceiling fans on Saturday. Just remember, Grams' birthday is on Sunday." It wasn't that Harley Bill was in favor of working on Sunday, but somehow Gramps sensed that the pressure of finishing the house might tempt him.

Mr. Bill nodded his understanding. With that they headed for their trucks and said goodnight.

Upon arriving at home, Mr. Bill discovered that Raelynn had already been tucked into bed, so he quietly slipped into her room to give her a goodnight kiss. Returning to the living room, the tired eleven-year-old boy was sent for his evening bath and instructed to get ready for bed. Settling down on the sofa beside his wife, he filled her in on the progress at the new house. "We'll be ready to install the lights and fans Saturday. The painters won't be there but all the ceilings will be finished. So what we do won't interfere with their progress. Gramps said he is free to help, and he's going to be there tomorrow evening to help finish the workshop. Why don't you and Raelynn come over about noon Saturday. Bring some lunch and we can go down by the creek for a picnic."

"That's a great idea, Harley," said Mrs. Bill. She was pleased that her husband would value some family time, especially since it had been very scarce lately. Of course she understood this, with the new house and all. "I'll call Grams and invite them to come along, okay." She shifted her position so she could look directly at him."Harley, you really look tired, why don't you go take your shower and turn in. I'll get Fossendocker to bed."

Smiling at her, he patted her hand, "I won't argue with that." He stood and headed down the hall. Pausing at the doorway to the bedroom that his boy's share he said, "goodnight, Dock, I love you, son, and hope you sleep well."

"Goodnight, Daddy, I love you, too, see you tomorrow," was the sleepy-sounding reply that came from the darkened room.

Mr. Bill smiled to himself. It appeared as though the boy had put himself to bed.

***

The next morning, Fossendocker's dreams of riding his bicycle as fast as the wind were interrupted by his mom's voice and a gentle shaking his of his shoulder. She was almost singing her words. "Time to wake up, time to wake up," When he finally opened his eyes, she gave him a kiss on the forehead, "I'll have your breakfast ready in a few minutes; how about a stack of blueberry pancakes and sausage?"

Sitting up in the bed, he remembered that just before he'd fallen asleep the night before, his stomach had growled. "I'm starved, Mom." Fossendocker scrambled from under his sheets and within minutes he'd washed his hands, dressed, and was at the breakfast table with his mom and little sister.

"I've got a lot to do around here today," his mother was explaining, "so I have a short list of things you can do to help." Getting up to pour herself another cup of coffee, she continued. "First of all. While I do a couple of loads of laundry, you can spend some time with Raelynn. There is a new book in her room. Let her read it to you and then help her with her spelling words. Then you can watch TV for a while as long as it's something educational."

Oh great, he thought, what a fun day this is going to be. It only took a few seconds for his discontentment to settle into an unhappy facial expression. It did not go unnoticed.

"Don't give me that look, I'm not through with you yet," said his mom. "Do you remember how you just crammed your cloths into your drawers yesterday?" The boy blinked, saying nothing. "You can just take it all out, refold them, and then put them all back in your drawers. *Neatly.* And I mean *all* of your drawers, in the dresser and the chest-of-drawers. Then we'll see if there's anything else you can help me with. Do you have any questions?"

The boy's shoulders sagged even lower, he shook his head indicating he had no questions, and silently ate his breakfast. He couldn't believe how poorly his life was going right now, and all because of that stupid old grease gun. However, Fossendocker followed his mother's plan to the letter; received a nod of approval for his reading and spelling assistance, and another nod for his choice of a nature show on the public TV channel. Mrs. Bill was so impressed with the tidiness of his drawers that she rewarded him with the task of folding the laundry she'd just done. It didn't much matter at this point what his mom made him do, anyway. He felt different, something inside felt different, like maybe he *should* start paying more attention to his parents. After all, they had told him that at least a million times. He didn't have time to dwell on this minor revelation very long, though. Time had flown by so fast that before Fossendocker knew it, his dad and he were back at the new house with Gramps working on the shelves and storage cabinets for the workshop.

"Say, Dock, I heard that we're going to do some picnicking down by the creek tomorrow," said his Gramps as he finished fastening a door-hinge onto the cabinet. "Anything to that? That's what Grams told me, but you never can tell about that ole woman." Gramps was smiling his big happy smile, and grabbed the boy in a headlock. Making a fist with his free hand, he lightly rubbed Fossendocker's skull with his knuckles. Gramps called this an Indian haircut, but Fossendocker knew it was just another way he had for showing affection toward his grandchildren.

"Yeah, Gramps," the boy yelled, still in the headlock. "Mom is fixing a potato salad. I know because I had to get the potatoes from the basement. And she's fixing ham sandwiches, too."

"That sounds mighty good, son, and while we're down at the creek, you and I will slip off upstream to the Devil's Elbow and check the fish traps I've got in there, okay." Fossendocker was nodding his approval, but did not interrupt his grandfather. "I put three baskets in the deep end of that hole the day before yesterday. Ought to have some fish in them by now, don't you think so?" Fossendocker still said nothing, but nodded again. "I'm about ready for a big batch of fried catfish, hush puppies, and some onion rings. Maybe I'll cook Grams some for her birthday. What ya think about that, Dock?"

Just as he was saying, "yeah, Gramps," his dad burst into laughter, and Gramps joined his son-in-law in a good hard laugh.

"You'll spend the rest of the summer in the barn with that goat of yours."

"You're right about that, Harley," both men laughed once again. "Your Grams does not care for fish, Dock. She won't cook it for me, and won't let me cook it in the house. But she does fix the best hush puppies and onion rings in the entire universe."

"Now I get it, Gramps," exclaimed Fossendocker. "You're just kidding about cooking fish for Grams." Kidding around like this was just one more reason why the boy was so close to his grandfather. Gramps loved to kid around and pull pranks on his friends and family. If he could get Grams wound up about something, that was even better. She almost always took his joking in good humor, explaining to her grandchildren that their Gramps couldn't help it because he was so full of nonsense.

For a long time Fossendocker thought that being full of nonsense was some kind of medical condition, until a few years ago when Ralph was kind enough to explain it to him. "What do you mean, 'is nonsense a disease?'" Ralph repeated his younger brother's question before bursting into laughter. "Of course it's not a disease, you moron. It just means that Gramps is full of bull."

"Then he's going to be alright?" inquired the younger brother with sincere concern. But to Fossendocker, being full of bull sounded almost as bad as being full of nonsense.

Ralph gave his little brother the impatient look that he had perfected over the past year or so. "Yes, he's going to be alright.

You know, Dock, to be as smart as you are, you sure can act like a real dummy sometimes."

Since that particular exchange, Ralph had taken the opportunity to be unkind to his younger brother on a number of occasions....a really high number of occasions. But Fossendocker had finally figured it out. As far as Ralph was concerned, he was simply the little brother that's always in the way, asking lots of questions, and in general, just being a pest. Now, he was just biding his time. He *would* get even someday. And he had the first installment at getting even, hidden in one of his comic books. The love-letter to Becky Boganthaul.

Becky, just happened to be the older sister of Brad Boganthaul, who just happened to be one of his and Leonard Lee Duvall's best buddies. And, to make matters worse, Becky, just happened to be a huge pain in the back side. She was constantly yelling at them for making too much noise, or whatever, when ever they were at Brad's house. As soon as he could go to Lenny's they would come up with a plan to have a little fun out of that love-letter. A little payback for Ralph *and* Becky.

BILL DALE GRIZZLE

CHAPTER 4

"Here's what I need for you to do, Fossendocker," said his dad, as he and Gramps were installing a ceiling fan. "When we finish in one room, you pick up all the trash, these little pieces of wire, everything, and put it in the empty box. Carry the box out to the dumpster, okay."

Fossendocker was carrying out his fifth box when his mom turned into the driveway. In the front seat was Grams, and Raelynn was safely buckled into the back seat. Running back into the house he cried out, "Mom and Grams are here!" That meant picnic time down by the creek.

Brightwell Creek, a free-flowing, clear, cold-water creek whose headwaters gurgle from the rocky cliffs of the Sagawata Mountains, flows from the northwest into the fertile farm land of western Collie County. In fact, Brightwell Creek and the mountains of the Sagawata Range were the very reasons that there is a Whitefox family in Collie County.

Gramps' own father, George William Whitefox, was born in 1915 in the low-lying lands of the Everglades of south Florida.

He'd grown up with stories of his People's People, as they were referred to. Verbal historical accounts, committed to memory and passed from one generation to another, of how his ancestors had chosen to leave their lands of rolling hills and clear, cold water. The People eventually made their way to the swamps of south Florida, rather than be forced by the white man to move out west. Here, they were safe and, for the most part, left alone to live their lives. When George Whitefox left the Everglade's and took a job with the railroad, he promised himself he would one day live on lands of rolling hills and clear, cold water, just as his ancestors had. Through years of hard work, much personal sacrifice, and saving every penny that he could, that promise to himself was kept. In 1940 George Whitefox married the lovely Miss Virginia LaFeaull, and together they bought the three hundred and two acres that lie on either side of Brightwell Creek.

At that time they had three neighbors, a dairy farm to their west, another dairy farm to their east, and the Federal Government. The Federal land was deemed the Sagawata National Forest in 1951. In 1976 Gramps and Grams bought the two hundred and fifty-three acre farm on the west side of the Whitefox property. The dairy farm had shut down three years earlier when there were no more family members interested in keeping it going.

On a knoll overlooking a horseshoe bend in Brightwell Creek, Gramps and Grams built their home. Here they raised their three children, and enjoyed a marriage that had lasted more than forty years. Now they are enjoying their grandchildren.

Before Gramps built this house, however, things were not so blissful for the young couple. They lived in the small, wooden frame house that George Whitefox built in 1940, with George and Virginia. When Gramps and Grams added to their family with their first and second child, Joseph David and Pearl Lucille, the little house was bursting at the seams. Thankfully, Gramps followed his father's example and advice, and within a few years they had their own place.

The little frame house sits empty now, although Gramps and Grams keep it clean and in good repair. Gramps' older sister, Aunt Anna, her family, and other family members, often stay there when they come to visit. Anna, according to Gramps, was a free spirit in her younger days. She moved away from Midway shortly after graduating from college and lived in a couple of different states before settling down in Texas. She stayed there, married a very nice man, and raised their children, but she comes home as often as she can.

Leaving the new house, the picnickers turned west onto the small county road. They traveled less than a half a mile and turned onto a dirt road just before crossing the creek. The gate at the little road was open already. "I stopped and opened the gate this morning, Grams, so you wouldn't have to get out." Fossendocker, sitting between his grandparents, smiled up at Grams knowing she would appreciate her husband's thoughtfulness. Just as she smiled back, Gramps hit a big bump in the road, and they both flew from the seat.

"You could slow down a little, Gramps, it's not like we're going to be late." But Grams knew he wasn't listening to her, all he was thinking about was getting to the creek.

"Is your daddy keeping up, Dock?" Gramps asked his grandson, who was looking out the back window. "Think your daddy's truck can handle this old creek road?"

"I hope so, Gramps," he said with concern in his voice, "Mom's got all the food."

That got a laugh from his grandparents. A few minutes later the road took a sharp turn to the left and the creek came back into view. After traveling a few hundred feet more, they pulled into a clearing about the size of two football fields.

As a boy, Gramps had spent much of his time in this clearing, a natural clearing that was then much less than half the size it is now. As a young man, he'd cleared the brush, vines, and cane that choked the little valley that's situated between Salter's

Ridge and the Six Cedar Hills, thus expanding the size of the clearing. Through the years Gramps had planted a variety of apple, pear, and cherry trees, and Grams had added her touch with Dogwoods and hundreds of azalea bushes. In the spring, Camp Seminole, as it had become known, was bursting with color and folks from all over the county would come to picnic and enjoy the outdoors. Gramps and Grams were generous people and were more than happy to share this part of their lives with their neighbors. The only thing they expected was that visitors let them know when they were coming, and help keep the place clean.

"Look at that, Grams," Gramps said excitedly, "somebody has cut the grass around the shelter and fire pit. Hey, they even put a coat of paint on the shelter. Folks sure are nice around here. Don't you think so Dock?" As a token of their appreciation, some of the local residents would help out with the upkeep of Camp Seminole. Most of the time Gramps wouldn't even know who had been there to lend a helping hand. He was always grateful, though, and always spread the word by saying so down at the hardware store, Miss Millie's Cafe, and at church. Word was sure to get around from those three places.

"I sure am ready for some lunch," remarked Grams. "I'm starving. I got up when you left this morning, Gramps, and cleaned the whole house, getting ready for tomorrow, you know." Grams never made a big deal about her birthday, or at least she tried not to let it show too much.

"*What*? What about tomorrow?" Gramps winked at Fossendocker. "Why tomorrow is just another Sunday, isn't it?" Fossendocker laughed as his grandmother smacked his grandfather on the thigh. Coasting to a stop just short of the shelter that covered four wooden picnic tables, they scrambled from the old pickup truck. All together they clapped their hands, cheered, and yelled, "*food*," as the rest of the picnickers rolled to a stop beside them.

Everyone pitched in and soon they were seated at one of

the big picnic tables enjoying ham sandwiches, potato salad, coleslaw, and iced tea. The conversation was lively and covered a variety of topics: The new house, the new schools, Grams' birthday dinner, and whatever else popped into their heads.

"Pearl Lucille Whitefox," Gramps exclaimed as he waved his fork around, "if you didn't learn anything else from your mother, you sure learned how to make a fine potato salad."

"Thank you, Daddy," she calmly answered, trying to keep a straight face, but it's Bill now. My name is Pearl Lucille Bill. It has been for a long time."

"Yeah, yeah, I know about that long time business. Your old mama and I will be married forty-two years come New Years Eve." Gramps gave Grams a wink and a smile. "That is unless I take a notion to run her off, beforehand."

Laughter echoed up and down Brightwell Creek.

"You're really going to get it Gramps," Mr. Bill chuckled. "With all that talk about fish yesterday, and now this, you'll be lucky to get to take your pillow to the barn with you."

"*What fish talk?*" Grams demanded, first looking at her son-in-law, then at her husband. "That senile old man knows I'm not going to cook him any fish."

More laughter rang out, as they dug into a plastic container of home made oatmeal cookies that Grams had baked the night before.

"The mayor over at Plainville called us the other day," said Gramps, as he chewed on a cookie, "to remind us about the big celebration at Miss Millie's Cafe on the twenty-eight of July. He knows how close Grams and Miss Millie are, and that Grams wouldn't miss it for the world."

Gramps paused and reached for another cookie. Anticipating this, Grams quickly moved the container out of his reach. Instead of a big oatmeal cookie, he got a handful of air, and a 'you've had enough' look. Having grown used to this over the past few years, he didn't give it any thought, and simply changed direction of his reach so he could give Raelynn a gentle pinch on the nose, before continuing on about Millie McCray. "Who would have thought she would have done so well selling nothing but chicken salad and that peanut butter goo. Stubborn old gal showed everybody, didn't she?"

"The Mayor says there is a student from Blakley University writing a book about her life," said Grams. "The girl's been coming all the way to Plainville every week for months. She spends two or three hours with Millie after she closes. I think she's working on her Masters Degree."

"I hope she does well," a sincere hopefulness was in Mrs. Bill's voice, "I would love to read that book."

"So would I, Pearl," her mother added. "You know she used to make fifty sandwiches everyday and take them to the automobile factory. She would leave the cafe at ten-forty-five, go sell her fifty sandwiches, and be back by eleven-thirty, ready for the lunch crowd."

Gramps winked at Fossendocker. "Your great-grandpa Whitefox worked at the auto factory, well, I mean at the railroad yard that was at the auto factory. One day that little Scottish lady really raked him over the coals for buying extra sandwiches and then selling them for a profit to the men who couldn't get out to her truck. She told him it wasn't fair to the others. She stood firm that her sandwiches were fairly priced, and recommended that he take care of keeping the trains on the tracks and she would take care of the sandwiches. And, to top it off, she limited him to two sandwiches per day. She then told him that if she heard about him selling them for a profit, his limit would be cut to zero."

Although his daughter and son-in-law had heard that story a dozen times, it was new to Fossendocker. He was fascinated and wanted to hear more. "What did he do, Gramps?"

"Well, Dock, the very next day he marched right up to that young lady and told her that she was absolutely right. He told her that he had worked hard all his life for what he had. Just like she was working hard to make something for herself. He apologized for overstepping his boundaries. Then my Daddy told her to stick to her good principals, and she would do just fine. And if she would trust him to do so, anytime any of his fellow workers couldn't get loose to go to her truck for a sandwich, he would get it for them, and never again make a profit. From that day forward they had a great respect for each other."

"Wow, Gramps, I sure am glad I'm in the Whitefox Clan," said Fossendocker.

"I am to, Dock, now let's go check those fish traps before we have to get back to work." Rising from the table, Gramps leaned over to kiss Grams on the cheek, but in a calculated move he quickly reached over and snatched two more cookies. "Got one for you, too, boy. Let's go." They hustled up the creek leaving Grams scolding in the background.

At the edge of the clearing, the pair stepped onto a well-worn trail and entered a stand of river cane so dense that after only a few steps they could no longer see Camp Seminole. The others may as well have been miles away. this was a different world.

Gramps stopped suddenly. "Listen here, Dock, let's keep our eyes peeled for ole no-shoulders, I saw a big Copperhead in here the other day."

Fossendocker nodded. He understood full well what his grandfather meant. "Gramps, why do you call snakes, no-shoulders?" His words were barely louder than a whisper.

"That's what my Daddy called them," Gramps replied. "And beside that, they've got no shoulders. You ever seen a snake with shoulders, Dock? Now let's go real quiet. Up ahead, when we get out of this cane break, look over to the other side of the creek. Up on that rocky ledge there's a little cave, It's just barely big enough for a fellow to get into. But I sure wouldn't get in it right now. A mama bobcat has got her three young ones in there. Good, safe place for raising those cubs. It's dry and pretty hard to get to."

The boy nodded again, as he studied the face of his

59

grandfather. He was always amazed how his Gramps knew so much, and he hungered for the life lessons he was taught each time they were together.

Once again Gramps stopped and knelt down, his gaze fixed on the far side of the creek. Any movement, regardless of how slight, would have been detected by his, still, sharp eyes. "No bobcats today," he whispered after several minutes. "We'll check again on the way out." The old man and his grandson continued making their way upstream.

"There's your favorite tree in the whole world, Gramps." Fossendocker ran ahead and climbed onto the lowest hanging limb. "How old is this tree, Gramps?"

"I really don't know, Dock. It doesn't seem any bigger now than when I was a boy. My Daddy always said that the Great Father might have stuck it here, full grown." He settled onto the ground and leaned back on the massive trunk of the old oak. "I spent a lot of time here when I was your age, Dock. Remember where I told you I found that big spear point?"

"I remember," answered Fossendocker. "It was under the old log by this tree, you were scratching around looking for worms to fish with, right? Where is that log, Gramps?"

Gramps chuckled, "Dock, that was more than fifty years ago. Shoot, that old log has long gone back to the mother earth. But it was right over there." He pointed and made a gesture to indicate the direction in which the fallen tree had landed. "I found a lot of arrowheads and pieces of pottery around here. It must have been a popular place for hunting, fishing, and camping back in the days of our ancestors."

A few moments of silence passed before Gramps spoke again. "Your mother tells me that you're having a hard time with this move to the new house. Anything to that, Dock?"

"Ah, you know, Gramps, I'm happy that we're going to be living close to you and Grams, but I'm going to miss Lenny and all my other friends. I'm not too happy about going to a new school, either."

Gramps could tell that his grandson was being honest and exposing his true feelings. He listened carefully as the boy express his concerns about moving to a new area, going to a new school, and making new friends. "Dock, you're going to have to do something I never did. I spent all my life right here on this land, except when I was in the Army. I was even able to live here while I attended college at Lincoln State. I never had to worry about moving to a new house, or going to a new school, or having to make all new friends."

Gramps caught hold of a nearby vine and pulled himself to his feet. He stretched, and stepped in front of his grandson. With the boy still on the limb, they were almost eye to eye. Placing his big rugged hands on his grandson's shoulders, Gramps took a long, deep breath before he spoke again. "Son, I'm not just going to say everything's going to be okay, although I'm pretty sure it will be. You're going to miss your old friends, and I'm sure that the new school will be a pain for a while. But you're a smart boy, and you have a good heart....I mean you know how to treat other folks. And I can tell you that those kind of qualities go a long way. Does that make any sense to you?"

"Clear as mud, Gramps," a smile replacing the worried look on Fossendocker's face. Gramps smiled back, and the boy could tell that his grandfather was pleased that he had used one of his favorite old sayings.

"And besides, boy, you'll have your old Gramps to fall back on for as long as the Great Father let's me walk on this earth."

"That's right, Gramps." The usual cheerful tone had returned to Fossendocker's voice. "We might have to get into some nonsense or something after we've become neighbors."

"You bet we will. In fact, soon as you get yourself off that restriction we're going to take the boat over to Pig's Eye Lake and catch us a bucket full of those big fat Blue Gill's. Just last week Mr. Yoder told me to come fish anytime I pleased."

Fossendocker and Gramps continued their hike upstream and within several minutes they reached the sharp bend in the creek, known as Devil's Elbow. Lying just downstream from the bend was the creek's largest pool. At fifty yards wide and almost twice that long, the water depth ranged from five feet to over twenty-five feet at the upper end. This pool, simply known as Big Hole, was without a doubt the best fishing hole on all of Brightwell Creek.

The little green boat was waiting safely on the bank of the creek. It was far enough from the water that it should be safe even if the area flooded, but securely tied to a tree, just to be certain. Gramps had this aluminum boat built some twenty-five or thirty years ago after the wooden boat that his father had built became so badly decayed that it was no longer safe to use.

Popping the top from a five gallon paint bucket, Gramps pulled out two life vest. Making sure that Fossendocker's vest was properly fastened, Gramps slid the boat into the creek. Fossendocker took his place in the back of the boat while Gramps settled into a specially designed seat in the very front. Using a paddle that was barley three feet in length, and paddling with only his left hand, he silently propelled the tiny craft across Big Hole. He never removed the paddle from the water, and the continuous figure-eight type motion hardly rippled the surface of the pool.

"About the time of the Civil War, our people in the Everglades learned to build boats very much like this one," explained Gramps, "and learned this technique of paddling. These wide, flat bottomed boats and this method of paddling worked well for them in the shallow, grassy waters of the swamps. My daddy taught me how to do this, and soon enough I'll teach you."

Reaching the first basket, Gramps grabbed the two-liter soft drink bottle that the traps stay line was tied to. Slowly he raised the basket from the creek bottom.

"Look, Gramps, we've got fish, three of them. One's kind of little, but the other two are keepers."

"Sure thing, boy," answered his grandfather, "let's throw that little one back, let him grow for a year or two. Bait's still good, so I'll let her back down."

The other two traps produced three more keepers, giving them a total of five for the day. Paddling over to a big rock that stuck out into the water, Gramps maneuvered the boat around it to the downstream side of the boulder. Here he had placed a big wire basket, a holding pen, as Gramps liked to call it. This basket was in a safe place, away from any current and floating objects that might cause damage to the wire sides. Gramps used the holding pen to keep his fish in until he had as many as he wanted.

"See you fellows real soon now," he said to the catfish as he dropped in the last one and closed the hatch. "I'll be back day after tomorrow to give you some of that fish food that I got at the hardware store the other day. It'll keep you fat and happy." Gramps stole a glance at his grandson; he seemed mesmerized that his grandfather would carry on a conversation with fish. "We want you to be fat and happy, we don't want to invite a bunch of skinny, unhappy catfish to our fish-fry. Right, Dock?" Fossendocker nodded, almost laughing out loud. "Let's head on back, Dock, we've been gone long enough. Grams might have a search party out looking for us."

"This sure has been fun, Gramps."

"Dock, I'm real proud that you show an interest in the outdoors and mother nature. On the outside you look like the Irish on your daddy's side and the Scandinavians on Grams' side. But as far as I'm concerned, you've got a full dose of Seminole on the inside. And what's inside is what defines a person, Dock. Always remember that."

They were still more than a hundred feet from the picnic tables where Fossendocker's parents and grandmother were seated, making small talk, when Grams shouted out. "How many of those smelly old catfish did you two catch?"

"Five keepers," Fossendocker shouted back, "put 'em in the

holding pen till we have enough for a big ole fish fry."

"Lord, Mama, the boy has even started to talk like Daddy," said Mrs. Bill in a quiet, but anxious sounding tone. "What in the world am I going to do with him? He's into everything and can tear up more stuff in a day than Harley can fix in a week!"

Grams grabbed Fossendocker as he approached the table. Wrapping her arms around her grandson she said. "Just got to love him." Next came a few sniffing noises. "You smell like a fish, Dock, go wash your hands before I have to get tough with you."

Mrs. Bill took a deep breath and let out a long sigh. She didn't hear a word I said, she was thinking, when she felt her mother's hand on her own.

"Pearl, just remember, you have to give out the love if you're going to give out the tough."

"I know, Mama, I know. We really hoped this restriction and making him work to pay for his daddy's grease gun, *and* the jeans he ruined, might cause him to think a little. But *noooo*, he falls in a ditch and breaks his glasses. I mean, I'm thankful that the only thing broken was his glasses. Heaven only knows how bad that could have been. But the bottom line is, Mama, had he not disobeyed his dad, that wouldn't have happened. And to top that off, we were both so relieved that he wasn't hurt any worse than a few scrapes, that we haven't addressed this yet."

"I know what you're saying, Pearl," Grams squeezed her hand, "he's a rambunctious little rascal."

"*Rambunctious?*" Mrs. Bill was trying hard not to raise her voice, "For crying out loud, Mother, he gave his little sister a shampoo with macaroni and cheese!"

Grams was putting serious effort into not bursting into laughter. "Well, he was only seven; no harm done, anyway, just look at that little doll." Raelynn was busy trying to catch a grasshopper. "Lucky for her, I taught you how to make a decent macaroni and cheese." Grams could no longer contain herself, and what started out as a snigger, mushroomed into a hardy laugh.

Feeling the glare from her daughter, who was not at all amused, she added. "It's too bad your Grandma's not here to give you some advice. She had to deal with your daddy when he was a boy."

Grams continued to laugh so loud that Gramps and Mr. Bill, who had strolled over to the creek bank, turned to see what all the fuss was about.

"Mama—," Mrs. Bill finally said, but she was cut off before she could say anything else.

"That's what you get for making him play house with his baby sister. Mind you now, I've never heard Dock complain very much about having to spend time with Raelynn, but he is a boy. So you'll get what you get with that deal."

"But it was pouring down rain that day, and I was cooking dinner for Harley's biggest customer and his wife. You know, the Acme Trucking Company guy, the guy that buys a gazillion tires from Harley every year.

"Yes, yes, I know all that," replied Grams. "Still, you know how that little angel follows her brother around like a puppy dog. So I'm just saying that if Dock told Raelynn that she should serve a cow pie, instead of a mud pie, at her next tea party.....you'd better look out."

"*Mother*, you're impossible!" Mrs. Bill had to laugh at that one. "I guess having lived with Daddy for forty years, some of his nonsense has rubbed off on you."

"I suppose so, Pearl." Grams cheerfully answered. "Now let's see if we can get those men back to work. Harley wanted to get all the lights and ceiling fans installed today, didn't he? Besides I need to get home and finish getting ready for tomorrow."

"Say, Ruby and the twins are supposed to be here around five o'clock, right?"

"Yep, their plane lands a little after two, so by the time they get out of the airport and pick up the rental car, I'm sure it will be at least five, maybe even five-thirty. I can't wait to see them. The girls are growing up so fast, just like Raelynn."

Ruby, the third child of Joseph and Helena Whitefox, is three years younger than her sister and five years younger than her brother. Throughout high school and college she had always told her parents that she wanted to be a school teacher. Her hearts desire was to work directly with Native American children. So at the tender age of twenty-two, with a college diploma in hand, she headed out west to her dream job. Three years later she married Thomas Two Eagles, two years after that the twins came along.

"It sure doesn't seem like ten years since Ruby moved out west." Mrs. Bill suddenly felt a pang in her chest, she missed her sister, sometimes much more than she would admit.

"Eleven, next month it will be eleven years," corrected her mother. "Thomas isn't coming with her this time. Ruby says he's got some issues at work to straighten out before the summer semester begins."

Dr. Thomas Two Eagles, a member of the Creek Nation, is the head of the history department at The University of Western Lands. By proving to the Whitefox Family that he was a trustworthy person, he solidified his place in the family. He further solidified his place by proving that he was a wonderful father to the twins, and whenever he couldn't make the trip to visit Ruby's family, he was sorely missed.

Grams and Mrs. Bill finished packing away all the picnic items and placed everything in the truck. "Harley, you and Fossendocker ride back with Daddy. I'm going to drop Mama off at her house. I'll see if she needs any help with anything before Raelynn and I head home." Her last sentence was spoken quietly as her husband approached, so that her fiercely independent mother wouldn't overhear and decline her help, even before it could be offered.

Mr. Bill wrapped his arms around his wife and gave her a big hug. "Thanks for a great lunch. This little break has really been good for me. If we get finished with this house and get moved in before I keel over, it will be a miracle."

"Don't work too late, okay," she stood on her tip-toes in order to give him a soft kiss, "you need to get some rest. I promise that I won't fuss if you decide not to go to church in the morning."

He smiled, gave her a wink, and then climbed into the cab of his father-in-law's old truck.

BILL DALE GRIZZLE

CHAPTER 5

It was going on ten o'clock the next morning when Harley Bill woke from an excellent night's sleep. He felt rested and refreshed, but did not get up immediately. Instead he took a few minutes to listen to the sweet sounds of laughter and chatter coming from his little girl. By the sound of it, her mom was getting her ready for church. Glancing at the clock on the bedside table, he realized they would be leaving any second for Sunday School.

Raelynn quickly looked up as her dad appeared in her bedroom doorway, "Daddy, you slept a lot." She broke free from her mother brushing her hair and ran for her dad's open arms. He lifted her over his head, which made her laugh even more. "Mommy said you're staying home today to rest and cook Grams' birthday dinner."

"Nice try, Mommy," said Mr. Bill, then gave Raelynn three quick kisses on the cheek. "Where's Dock?"

"He's sitting in the living room. He's been ready for half an hour," answered his wife while shaking her head. "He hasn't said a word since breakfast, he just got ready and sat down in the living room. Kind of strange?"

Returning Raelynn to the floor, Mr. Bill shrugged his shoulders and delivered a soft kiss to his bride's cheek. "Who knows what's strange when it comes to a kid that's growing up as fast as he is. The coffee sure smells good and I'm ready for a cup."

"I just made a fresh pot. I figured you would be getting up soon," replied Mrs. Bill as she put the finishing touches on Raelynn's hair. "And there are blueberry muffins, too. How about keeping an eye on that ham in the oven. The timer is set, so all you have to do is take it out when the timer dings. Now, it's time for us to go."

Goodbye hugs and kisses were brief as Mrs. Bill quickly shuffled her children out the front door and into the SUV. "Oh, and, Harley, don't forget to turn the oven off."

Mr. Bill stood at the front door and watched as his family disappeared around the corner before heading for the kitchen and that cup of coffee. He had just sat down at the table with his coffee and a pair of muffins when he was interrupted by the dogs racing through the kitchen to the back door. Duke and Duchess, brother and sister, West Highland White Terriers. They both slid to a stop and sat motionless looking up at the door.

"Alright," Mr. Bill finally said. He had just taken the last bite of his first muffin when Duke let out an impatient little bark. As he opened the door, the pair shot out right into the path of Patches, their nine-year-old cat. Caught completely by surprise, every hair on the poor cat's body stood on end, and she gave both Westies a sharp slap as they sped by.

"Get 'em, Patches! Exclaimed Mr. Bill, laughing at the cat, "Don't let those crazy dogs run over you." He let the otherwise maintenance free calico in and put fresh food in her bowl.

"Fee da cat, fee da cat!" The loud, shrill, and equally demanding voice of Julio, the bird, struck his ears and caused him to jump with surprise.

"I should feed you to the cat," he said under his breath, as he opened the cage to put bird seed into his bowl. Much to his dismay, however, his hand was met by a swift, hard, peck from Julio's sharp beak. "*Ouch, you little*....if you were big enough I'd fry you up and eat you myself! You're one ungrateful bird."

On the next attempt, by exercising caution, Mr. Bill managed to deliver the bird seed without suffering further damage from Julio's weapon. "There, I'm finished with you." He closed the door on the bird cage and strolled to the sink to wash his hands and inspect the half-inch long cut on the back of his hand. "Just how long do birds live, anyway?" He muttered a few more threats to the bird before once again turning his attention to his breakfast.

***

As Mrs. Bill neared the driveway of the church parking lot, she asked, "Fossendocker, sweetheart, are you alright, you haven't spoken in forty minutes?"

"Mom, can I at least sit with Lenny at church?" The request was made as humbly as possible. Since he had long figured out that the one driving could see him in the rear-view mirror, he also wore a pitiful, pleading expression in his eyes.

"It's, may I, and yes, you may," answered his mother, stealing a quick glance at him in the rear-view mirror, "but no funny business, is that clear."

Her voice was stern, so the boy knew he had better be careful in executing his plan. The very reason for his silence all morning was securely stuffed into his pants pocket. His older brother's love-letter. Fossendocker intended to share this find with his best friend so they could figure out just what to do with it. But how was he going to pull this off in such a public place, knowing that Leonard would bust a gut laughing?

The *bathroom*, Fossendocker thought, that's the perfect place. Mom can't watch me in there, and Dad's not here. His mother was hardly parked when he bailed out of the car and

71

headed for his Sunday School classroom.

"Remember what I said, young man." His mother's words almost didn't register in his preoccupied brain.

"Yes, ma'am."

Leonard Lee Duvall was already in the Sunday School classroom when Fossendocker burst into the room.

"Good to see you're so anxious for today's lesson, Dock," jabbed Patty Payne, the twenty-year old college student and future teacher. "You and Lenny both here on time, now that's a minor miracle."

Fossendocker waved off her comments and rushed to his seat next to Leonard. "Hi Lenny, how's it going?"

Leonard didn't say anything for a few seconds, he just stared at his best friend. "Are they making you wear those glasses, Dock? That's mean."

"*No*," snapped Fossendocker, giving his friend a frown. "I picked them out myself; got two pair just alike."

Leonard continued to stare.

"Stop looking at me. You'll get used to 'em," Fossendocker said with confidence. "Now listen to me Lenny, I have something in my pocket that you're not going to believe. I can't show you now, not here. But when Sunday School is over and before church starts we'll go to the bathroom and I'll show you."

Pure curiosity was killing Leonard. The forty-five minutes of Sunday School seemed like half a day. "Come on Lenny, let's go to the bathroom in the fellowship hall, it'll be more private there."

With the bathroom door securely locked behind them, Fossendocker pulled the letter from his pocket, unfolded the paper and handed it to Leonard. Somewhat confounded, Leonard just looked at the page. Actually he was expecting to see some kind of insect, or a lizard, or something, not a sheet of paper.

"*Read it*, Lenny." His friends impatience jolted Leonard. "You're going to love this. I found it under the bed while I was cleaning my bedroom."

Leonard read the words aloud, "'Dear Becky, I'll be moving to Midway soon and I will miss you so much.....'" And then just like his best friend had done a few days before, he stopped and his eyes went to the bottom of the page. There was the big heart with an arrow through it, and all those X's and O's. "This is to Becky Boganthaul!" Leonard almost shouted and burst into laughter.

Fossendocker could no longer hold it and he, too, burst into laughter. The noise the two boys were making, while laughing and making crude comments about Ralph and Becky and what a pain in the neck they both were, soon gained the attention of the outside world. Someone knocked on the door, and a deep, male voice asked. "Is everything alright in there?"

"*Yes sir*," they both exclaimed, as Fossendocker grabbed the letter from Leonard, refolded it, and stuffed it back into his pocket.

"When I get off restriction, we'll figure out what to do with this letter," said Fossendocker. "Come on, we'd better get to the church. This is our secret, Lenny, don't you dare tell anybody. Don't even tell Brad. If Ralph finds out, he'll kill me for sure."

"Okay, Dock." It was almost always, 'okay, Dock.' Leonard had allowed Fossendocker to lead him down the road of trouble virtually since the day they'd learned to walk. This was shaping up to be another one of those trips down that proverbial road.

***

"What happened to your hand, Harley?" Mrs. Bill noticed the band-aid on the back of his left hand as they were turning into the driveway of her parent's home.

"That *bird* of yours pecked a chunk of meat out of it, that's what," was his matter-of-fact answer. But, his look of disgust told his true feelings for the bird *and* of being pecked. Mrs. Bill was very aware of the ongoing conflict between her husband and the

73

temperamental bird, but still, she was not going to take this dig sitting down.

"What did you do, Harley, threaten to feed him to the cat again?" She barked. "Good enough for you, if you did. Oh look, everybody, there's Ruby coming out to meet us."

Ruby Whitefox Two Eagles bounded from the front porch and ran toward the approaching car. Opening the passenger door as soon as Mr. Bill had turned the engine off, she threw her arms around her sister as she was trying to get out of the car.

"No matter how long I live out west, I still miss my family." Ruby choked back happy tears. "I miss you all the same now as I did when I first moved out there." She held onto her older sister long enough for everyone else to get out of the car.

"Let me look at you, Ruby," said Mrs. Bill, backing up just far enough to focus on her little sister's face. Ruby's long, straight, almost jet-black-hair, blew in the gentle breeze, and her clear green eyes sparkled like emeralds against her reddish-brown complication.

"Ruby, I'll swear girl, you have never looked better in your life. I'm so jealous. You've got our mother's beauty, and our father's handsomeness, all rolled up into one package."

"You're much too kind, sister." Ruby blushed, looking at the ground. "Besides, I've always been a little envious of your blond hair and those killer blue eyes."

"Maybe so, Ruby, but blue-eyed blonds are a dime a dozen. But you have that look that women would die for. And I'm so glad that the twins favor you so much."

"That they do," nodded Ruby, "right down to the eye color." Ruby took the platter which held the baked ham, securely wrapped in aluminum foil, from the back seat of the car. "Let me help out. Boy, this sure smells good!"

"Hello, Dock. Hello, Raelynn." Ruby winked at them both. "I'll get my hugs and kisses when we get inside. Harley, how are you doing?" Ruby never failed to speak to everyone at any kind of function, from the oldest down to the youngest, causing them to feel warm and welcome. This genuine gift had served her well since relocating out west. In eleven short years she had elevated herself from a first grade teacher to the principal of the largest elementary school in the district. "Daddy says that you should have the new house ready to move into within the next few weeks."

"I'm doing fine, thank you," replied Mr. Bill. "The plan is to be settled in before school starts. If nothing goes wrong, we should make it."

"I'll get Daddy to take me over there tomorrow. I'm so happy for you two, and I know Mama and Daddy are going to love having you all living so close to them. By the way, where's Ralph?"

"He's coming with our brother," answered Mrs. Bill, "he's been at their house visiting for a week."

"Well," her younger sister added, "Opal called a few minutes ago saying they're going to be a little late. Thurson dropped the tea, so she's making another gallon. Come on in and see how these girls have grown."

"Girls, come here please, Aunt Pearl and Uncle Harley are here." As the twins hurried into the living room, she added, "and Dock and Raelynn."

"*Holy smokes*," shouted Mr. Bill, "These girls are about grown!"

"I'll say they're about grown!" exclaimed Gramps, "I figure they'll need to be looking for a job pretty soon. What do you think Raelynn?"

The twins, Faith and Henna, were giggling, but Raelynn was very serious with her answer. "*No*, Gramps, they're not big enough yet. See, they're the same size as me." She backed up to one of the twins so Gramps could see for himself.

"Well," replied Gramps, speaking louder than normal, using his jolly-sounding voice, so even the youngest grandchild would know that he was joking. "*You're all growing up too fast, and I want you to stop it!"*

With everyone getting a laugh out of Gramps' comment, Faith, Henna, and Raelynn took off for the backyard. The ladies headed for the kitchen, Mr. Bill flopped onto the couch, and Fossendocker took a seat in the floor beside his Grandfather's recliner.

"Hey, Gramps." Fossendocker was looking upward so he could see Gramps as he leaned over the arm of the chair.

He reached out and gave the boy a quick Indian haircut, getting in just one swipe before Fossendocker dodged out of the way. "What is it, squirt? Why don't you come up here and sit with me. That way I can give you a proper haircut." He was reaching for the boy who kept squirming out of his very loose and playful grasp.

"No way, Gramps." Fossendocker laughed and squirmed some more. "I don't need a haircut."

"You're just a squirt, Dock," joked Gramps. "I'll decide when you need a haircut....you need one now!" He grabbed the boy, dragged him into his lap, balled up his fist, and gently buffed the top of Fossendocker's fuzzy-blond head with his knuckles. The boy was laughing hysterically, flailing like a fish out of water, and making it very difficult for Gramps to hold him.

With the haircut completed, Gramps held the boy at arms-length to inspect his handiwork. "That's better now, Dock, you look real presentable."

Being presentable. That was another thing that Gramps was very particular about. Realizing that he didn't have the keenest fashion sense, Gramps would always ask Grams, if he was presentable. He had no desire to be an embarrassment to Grams or himself whenever they were out in public. Of course, Grams always made sure that he looked nice.

"Okay, Gramps," Fossendocker warned, "someday when I'm big enough, I'm gonna to give you an Indian haircut."

Gramps laughed, running his hand over his still coal-black

hair. "I just hope that I have some hair left by then. It feels like it's gettin' kinda thin up there. Grams says there's some gray ones around the sides, too, but I think she's just seeing things."

"Gramps, when Ralph and Thurson gets here, will you tell us a story about the old days? You haven't told us a story in a long time, please, Gramps." Ralph and Thurson had pretty much lost interest in the stories Gramps told about his ancestors, when they reached their teen years, but not Fossendocker. He could listen to those stories for hours on end. Stories that had been passed from generation to generation by the spoken word. All of the names, places, dates, all of the details, everything, was committed to memory.

Fossendocker had high hopes that his Grandfather would teach him all of the stories, and he hoped he could remember them all. He found it odd and confusing that his own mother did not really enjoy the stories. She would listen politely, but would never attempt to repeat any of the tales. Truth be known, she had never felt connected to her father's people the way she did to her mother's side of the family. And Uncle J.D., try as he might, could never get a story straight. If Gramps was not around to lend him guidance, he would always decline the opportunity to tell of their ancestors. Aunt Ruby, though, much to the delight of her father, had mastered the art of telling stories. She had memorized every story that Gramps had ever told, right down to the smallest detail, and then she would add her own personal touches to them. For example: her story could be about a young warrior slipping through the swamps in pursuit of game. Ruby would include details about the smells and colors of the various flowering plants, the faint swishing of the reeds as the young man's thigh pushed them aside, or the ever so slight ripple made by an alligator as it slips beneath the surface of the swampy waters. However, these embellishments were not just fabrications of her imagination. She had visited the Everglade's at least a dozen times, and had read every book she could get her hands on concerning the Seminole

People.

Even at the tender age of eleven, Fossendocker knew that his grandfather would find great favor in him if he grew up to be the kind of story teller that his Aunt Ruby had become.

Gramps loved his three children equally, but he couldn't help feeling a little closer to Ruby than the other two. It was a spiritual thing, and he had the very same feelings toward the mischievous little grandson that was presently sitting on his knee. He had felt this closeness the moment this boy was born, and it had never faded.

"Tell you what, Dock," Gramps finally said, "after we eat, I've got a good one to tell you, okay."

Fossendocker gave his grandfather a wide grin, nodded like a bobble-head doll, and politely said, "okay, Gramps." He hopped off his grandfather's knee and started for the kitchen to check on dinner, when his little sister burst into the room, followed closely by his cousins, Faith and Henna.

"Uncle J.D. is here!" shouted Raelynn.

"Good," stated Gramps, "about time! That boy will be late for his own funeral. Besides that....," he grabbed Raelynn and gave her a big hug, "Grams made me eat a bowl of oatmeal for breakfast and I'm about to starve!"

"Me too, Gramps," said the little girl, as Gramps returned her to the floor. She and the twins rushed back to the kitchen.

Gramps was watching J.D. and his family approach the front steps when he overheard Grams scolding the grandchildren in the kitchen. "Why don't we see if we can get a few more grand kids in here, we've got plenty of room, ya know." He had to chuckle when one of them said, "okay." Apparently they didn't understand her humor, or her subtle scolding.

Holding the storm door open, J.D. allowed his wife, Opal, and his sixteen year old daughter, Jewel, to enter the house. Thurson and Ralph were lagging behind, so J.D. stepped in and let the door close behind him.

Exchanging hellos, hugs, and handshakes, Gramps found himself thinking that his son was an alright kind of guy. He may not be able to remember the family stories, but at least he did remember to hold the door for the ladies. Gramps was proud of his oldest child, he'd done well for himself in spite of the fact that he only completed one year of college. Opting instead for a vocational education, J.D. opened a small machine shop in Lincoln. He now has a half-dozen full-time employees, had landed a number of lucrative government contracts, and was doing quiet well for his family.

Thurson and Ralph finally came through the front door, one carrying a covered dish, the other a gallon jug of tea. Opal gathered the dish and the tea into her arms and headed for the kitchen.

"Hey, boys," said Gramps, "gimmie five." He was holding out both hands expecting both boys to slap his palms.

"Ah come on, Gramps, man, that is so lame," said Thurson. "Nobody does that anymore."

"Yeah, Gramps," added Ralph, "now we say, gimmie some knuckles, or get ya some of this."

Both boys made a fist with their right hands and gently bumped their knuckles together. "Just like this," instructed Ralph. And just like that, Gramps had received an up-to-date education on proper greetings.

Feeling a little confounded, Gramps first looked at his son, then at his son-in-law. Both men simply shrugged their shoulders. "Okay, then," he finally said as he made fists with both hands, "hey, boys, get ya some of this."

"Yeah, Gramps, that's it," muttered Thurson, as both boys tapped their fists to the fists of their grandfather. With that, both boys started toward the kitchen.

Mr. Bill cleared his throat, causing Ralph to look in his direction. His glance was met by a disapproving stare from his father.

"Oh. Hi, Dad, how's it going?" They continued on into the

kitchen, hoping for a nibble, but instead found themselves being escorted to the back door by their grandmother. Even their 'Happy Birthday' wishes failed to prevent them from being expelled to the backyard.

"Go find Dock," said Grams. "Dinner will be ready in ten minutes, and he's probably down at the barn with that smelly old goat. Get him back up here so Gramps can say thanks to the Great Father."

Topping the rise between the house and the barn, Ralph could plainly see his little brother, both hands with a firm grip on the goat's horns, engaged in a game of tug-of-war, back and forth across the barnyard.

"*Oh, great*," complained Ralph, "he's going to smell like a goat for the rest of the day. And I'll have to ride in the car with him. I may go back home with you, Thurs." Ralph sat down on the thick grass and leaned back against the big apple tree. Picking up a twig he started breaking it into short pieces and tossing each one at a honey bee, as it busily checked the blossoms of a nearby patch of clover.

"Hey, Dock," Thurson called out loud enough to be heard, "Grams said it's time to eat."

With that, Fossendocker let go of the goat's horns and raced for the fence. He narrowly escaped a farewell nudge from Scooter, who was in hot pursuit. Then he hustled toward Thurson and his brother. It'll be good to see Ralph, he said to himself, a part of him had actually missed his older brother, or so he thought. At twenty paces he stopped in his tracks as Thurson broke into laughter. His cousin was poking Ralph, who was still tossing pieces of the twig at the honey bee, and pointing in his direction. *Now what*, wondered Fossendocker.

Apparently Ralph didn't know what to say when he finally looked up at his brother. For several seconds he just stared. "Dock, what the....are those things *real*?"

"Are what real?" the dumbfounded Fossendocker asked.

80

"Those goofy-looking glasses, you dork. Are they real?" Ralph had now joined Thurson in laughter which, naturally, sent Fossendocker's anger level through the roof. Breaking into a run, he passed the laughter of his big brother and cousin and didn't slow until he reached the back door of his grandparent's house.

Ralph and Thurson watched, still laughing hysterically, as Fossendocker sped over the rise toward the house. "I guess they're real," choked Thurson, giving Ralph a slap on the back. "That's your kid brother, Ralph"

"Yeah, well, please don't remind me," sputtered Ralph, "I'll swap him for your sister. At least she's quiet."

Fossendocker let the screen door slam behind him as he entered the house, stopped, returned to the door and closed it properly. All the ladies in the kitchen looked at him with wonder. He was extremely red-faced, huffing and puffing.

"What's the matter with you, Dock?" His mother stepped forward, questioning his behavior. "What's wrong?"

"*Ralph, that's what....,*" he yelled, "Ralph and Thurson are making fun of me; laughing at my new glasses." Fossendocker shot into the family room, the safe haven, where his Gramps sat in his favorite recliner. He wouldn't let the big kids pick on him. There he sat, within easy reach of the one person in the whole wide world he most trusted with his deepest inner feelings. Occasionally glancing up at his Gramps for reassurance, he dreamed of ways he could get even with his pesky older brother, and that cousin of his, Thurson.

Several minutes later Grams called everyone to the dining room, where the table was loaded with food and drink. Before anyone took a bite, though, Gramps would speak with the Great Father.

Joseph Whitefox, had all his life been a person of deep faith, as had his father, and his father's father. The knowledge of God and his Son, Jesus, had been delivered to his people many decades earlier. As a youngster, Gramps had given his heart to God and he'd decided to live his life according to the teachings of the Holy Bible. Like all his ancestors, he referred to God as the Great Father, and Jesus as the Blessed Son. The mingling of ancient traditions into his worship might seem odd, or even a little confusing to those who did not know Joseph Whitefox. But to those who did know him, it was perfectly acceptable. Gramps placed great importance on the role of nature in our lives, the earth, water, the sun, and the balance between mankind and all the other creatures under God's far-reaching hand. Gramps placed even greater importance on what he was to do with the time that he is given on this earth. All these things were gifts from the Great Father, not to be worshiped, but never to be taken for granted, either. Nonetheless, he was quick to offer up prayers for anyone in need of prayer and just as quick to offer up words of thankfulness.

Gramps stepped to the table, looked upward, and after several seconds he appeared to be looking through the ceiling, through the roof even, and straight into the eyes of his Creator. Slowly raising his arms, hands open, palms up, to just above shoulder height, he spoke. "Great Father," his deep voice boomed through the dining room. "We are grateful for your Spirit that lives in our hearts; we are grateful for your Spirit that walks with us. We are grateful for our family and this bounty. Great Father, we are grateful for all that you have created, and for all that you have allowed us to use during our days on this earth." Lowering his hands and looking down at the table, a huge smile spreads across his leathery, reddish-brown, yet still handsome face. "Amen. Let's eat." Suddenly everyone was talking at the same time, and joy rang out in their voices.

The Whitefox house was not a big house. Joseph William Whitefox and Helena Gustoff Whitefox did not see the need for such a huge dwelling. The four bedrooms and the two bathrooms were relatively small, with the master bedroom being only slightly larger than the other three. The living room, or family room as it was always called, with its rock fireplace and vaulted ceiling, seemed much larger than it actually was. Nonetheless, there was always ample room for everyone with the addition of a few dining room chairs.

The two areas they did splurge on were the kitchen and the dining room. Gramps felt like it was very important for Grams to have a spacious, comfortable kitchen, with plenty of cabinets, counter space, a pantry big enough for a freezer, and all the modern conveniences. Of course, that was just fine with Grams, as was the oversized dining room that Gramps had insisted on. According to his calculations, if all three of their children had three children each, there would be enough room for in-laws, grandchildren, and maybe even some great-grandchildren. He even had the talented craftsmen at Scottish Furniture Works, a local producer of handcrafted furniture, build them a fine table to fit the space.

"Open ours next, Grams." Fossendocker placed the gift box in her hands then rushed back to his seat so he could watch. Dinner had been eaten, *Happy Birthday* had been called out and sang, the cake had been cut, and now presents were being opened.

"Why thank you, Dock, thank you all so much, you shouldn't have." Grams picked at the tape, trying not to tear the paper.

"It's not much, Mama," said Mrs. Bill. "But we had to get you something, even though you always say that you don't need a thing."

Grams finally got the paper off and opened the box. Peeking inside she actually looked surprised. "Well I'll be. Something I didn't have." Grams pulled out a smaller, unwrapped package. "Look Gramps, an indoor-outdoor thermometer. This part stays in the house and this part goes outside." She was pointing to the picture on the packaging. "That way you can tell how cold it is without sticking your head out the door. And look, that book I told you I wanted on the birds of North America." She held up the book for everyone to see. "Thank you all so much."

"I picked out the thermometer, Grams," said Fossendocker with a certain degree of satisfaction in his voice. "I picked it out at Mega-Mart the same day I picked out my new glasses."

Once again Ralph and Thurson burst into laughter. "*You* picked them out?" sputtered Ralph. "I figured Mom made you. Man, you look like a real geek."

Before either Mr. or Mrs. Bill could say anything to their oldest son, their youngest sprang from his chair and yelled almost as loudly as he could. "It's okay if I look like a Greek!" The boy was pointing his finger directly at Ralph. "Gramps had glasses like this a long time ago. If it was okay for Gramps to look like a Greek, then it's okay for me to look like a Greek, too."

Ralph and Thurson both stopped laughing, obviously surprised by Fossendocker's outburst. He was still standing between the table and the chair he had been sitting in, coldly staring at his older brother.

The dining room had fallen silent. Everyone had turned to look at the red-faced Fossendocker, wondering what might come next. Then from the far end of the table, the normally very quiet Opal said, with a definite question in her voice, "*GREEK?*"

Everyone older than Fossendocker erupted into laughter, leaving him wondering what was so funny about that. Gramps seized the moment to congratulate him for standing up for himself, thus avoiding additional outburst, and soon the table returned to normal. Grams had two more presents to open, including the big one from Gramps. They all knew it was one of those new vacuum cleaners, the kind that's not supposed to loose suction.

"Now Mother, you just sit down and take it easy." Ruby escorted Grams to her favorite old wing-back chair. Waiting for her to take a seat, she added. "It's your birthday, so we'll take care of all the clean up." On her way back to the kitchen she said, "J.D., Harley, I appreciate your helping, too."

"You see how she does," said J.D. shaking his head at his brother-in-law, "she makes it sound like we've already done something. So now if we don't help, we really look like jerks."

Without responding, Mr. Bill headed for the dining room and began clearing the table. Several seconds later J.D., feeling a little lazy after such a big meal, managed to pull himself from the couch and follow.

Knowing that Gramps wouldn't begin his story until all were seated in the family room, Fossendocker busied himself sorting through the dozens of arrowheads, spearheads, and scraping tools that his grandfather had found along the banks of Brightwell Creek. He held one, then another, in his hands, allowing his mind to wonder about each one's place in history. Was this one used for hunting? Was this one used in battle? There was no way to tell, but nonetheless he enjoyed holding them, touching them. When he came across his favorite arrowhead, he sat down on the floor beside Gramps' old brown leather recliner to patiently wait for the story to begin. Staring at his hands, he opened them just enough to peek at the ancient stone point, then once again closed them tightly.

"This is the story of Micco Sando who came to this earth in the white man's year 1841, and left this earth in the white man's year 1922, when he had lived eighty-one circles around the sun. He was the son of the great warrior, Talahtal Micco, whose name is said to mean two great cats. Micco Sando was the father of my grandfather, and the first of many to be called Whitefox.

The young boy, still cradling the arrowhead in his tightly closed hands, was wide eyed and all ears. He was well pleased that Gramps was telling the story of how the name, Whitefox, had originated. It had been two or three years since this story had been told, and much to his dismay, he had forgotten most of it.

"As you know, the People decided to move farther south rather than be forced to move westward. The pressure from the white man and the American Government had become great. It had become more than they could bear. South Florida became their new home around 1830, and with a new home, came a new way of life. In spite of more than fifty years of on-again, off-again wars with the government, the People thrived in their new home. With each passing season, their knowledge of their lands grew and they became wise to the ways of the marsh lands."

"By the time Micco Sando had become a young man, there were no more wars with the white man. Peace had long since been made with the American Government and, for the most part, the People were left alone to live their lives. They did well in the swamps and thickets of the Everglades, and the lands around the swamps. All sorts of food was plentiful, a wide array of plants, berries, and fruits were at their disposal. Plus, growing crops in the fertile soil outside of the swamps proved to be productive. More importantly, all kinds of game, waterfowl, fish, and shellfish were also plentiful. The People learned more and more about how to hunt and fish these lands, and waters and Micco Sando was considered among the best. Much could be told about this courageous young man, but that is another story for another time. But I will tell you that he became a master at trapping, both fish and game. The People credit him with building the first fish traps, the kind that are still in use to this very day."

"Wow, Gramps," blurted out Fossendocker. "Are they the same kind of traps we've got in Big Hole?"

"Yes, they are, Dock." Gramps didn't mind the interruption at all, because he knew the boy was not only listening, he was excited about what he was hearing. "The only thing different is what they're made out of. We use metal screen and wire now, instead of cane, reed, and strips of leather. They last a lot longer nowadays." Gramps reached out and playfully rubbed the top of his grandson's head, letting him know that he approved of his curiosity.

"Micco Sando also began using a different kind of trap for small animals, muskrat, mink, raccoons, and the like. It is not clear how he came to use such traps. I can not say with certainty that our ancestor invented these traps. He may have learned of them from some far away people, but I can say with certainty that he was the first of our People to use these traps. They were built from cane, with a trap door, and looked kind of similar to the rabbit boxes I built when I was just about Dock's age. Once a critter would go into the trap for the bait, a door would close. The animal would be caught, but it would not be harmed. Now, I would like to say that he was being thoughtful of the animals but, the fact of the matter is, he did not want to damage the critter's hide. Not only was this food for the People, the hides were used for shoes, pouches, storage bags, and other articles of clothing. They were also traded to other people and to the white man for things they needed."

Gramps stopped for a sip of his tea, glancing around the room. He couldn't help noticing that even Raelynn, sandwiched between the twins, was paying attention. Most of the time her mind was too active to devote much time to a story. "Now here is where the real story begins," said Gramps, sliding to the edge of his seat.

"It was late Spring, so the story goes, and Micco Sando was checking his traps one sunny day. As he silently approached the trap that he had set at the edge of a clearing, a clearing that had been made by a storm when many trees were blown down, he could see that he had caught something. Creeping closer to get a better view, the young hunter was caught completely by surprise by what was in his trap. Indeed it was a fox, and a fox was a worthy catch for any trapper, but this fox was like no other that he had ever seen. Its coat was as white as an egret and its eyes as blue as the skies above him. Slipping still closer, it became obvious that this was a female fox that was caring for a litter of pups. She never panicked at the approaching human, she simply watched his every move with great concern. Micco Sando was quiet certain he had never seen an animal as beautiful as this fox, and he knew her pelt would be very valuable. Still, he hesitated to dispatch the critter, and he made the faithful decision to release her. Opening the door of the trap, the fox raced away but stopped after only a hundred feet or so and hid behind a palmetto bush. She was not hidden as well as she thought, though, because her white fur was shining brightly in the sun. Micco Sando knew that her den must be nearby. Many times that day, as he continued to check his other traps, his mind wondered if he had made the right choice. Surely he would never again have the opportunity to hold a white fur in his hands, but his heart held no regrets.

"When he returned to his village he told the story of the white fox with the blue eyes to all who would listen. Some believed the story, some did not. Believing that truthfulness was the mark of a man, this was not good enough for the young hunter. He wanted others to see this creature. So he convinced two men who did not believe his story to go with him to watch the clearing, in hopes of seeing the white fox once again. After many hours their patience was rewarded when the fox appeared from nowhere and hopped up onto a great log."

"Soon this story was known far and wide by all the People, and it was known to be the truth. Many others saw the white fox, and it was learned that she had five pups, two of which were white. To this very day there are white foxes in the swamps of south Florida, the offspring's of that first white fox, and they are protected by the People."

"The next year, Micco Sando took as his bride a beautiful young woman, Lafawn Minlitto, whom he had known since childhood. In those days it was customary for the new husband to leave his village and move into the new wife's village, becoming part of her family. At the wedding ceremony, though, the Chief of the People broke tradition and proclaimed that there would be a new family. He spoke into law, that, 'Micco Sando shall forever be known as Micco Sando Whitefox, and his children shall be known as Whitefox, and his children's children shall also be known as Whitefox.'"

Gramps settled back into his recliner and took a deep breath. All eyes were fixed on him. "So that's why to this very day there are still Whitefoxes, not only in the Everglades, but here, and in Texas, and Oklahoma, and other places....the offspring's of that very first Whitefox."

As Gramps looked about the room, smiling faces told of the family's approval of the story they'd just heard. But, he had more to say. "The name Whitefox is a worthy name, given to a worthy man, and passed down to us. Like the white foxes of the swamps, protected by the People, the name Whitefox must also be protected by the People. We must always be mindful that *we are* the People."

Now that Gramps was finished, most of the adults were nodding in agreement. It was then that Ruby jumped to her feet and rushed to give her dad a big hug and tell him he had told a wonderful story. This spurred other comments about how they had enjoyed the story, too.

Once again the young boy opened his hands to stare at the arrowhead. Looking up at his grandfather, he realized that he was being watched. Gramps smiled at him. "That was a great story, Gramps, thanks for telling it to us. I really like that story." Gramps smiled again and gave him a wink. Rising to his feet, Fossendocker made his way across the family room and placed the arrowhead back into the box with the others.

"Gramps, may I ask a question." Jewel was as quiet as her mother so the request caught her grandfather by surprise. "Why don't you ever tell stories about the women in the family? I'd like to learn about the women."

"You're right, Jewel, you need to know about the women in our family. No doubt, this family would be a skeleton of itself if not for its great women. While your Aunt Ruby is here you should get her to tell the story of Virginia LaFeaull. Her grandmother and my Mother. Ruby spent a lot of time with her grandmother and probably knows more about her life than I do. And, she tells the stories so well. How about it Ruby?"

"Yeah, Aunt Ruby," Jewel said with excitement in her voice. "I can just barely remember Grandmother Virginia, since I was only like five when she passed away."

Ruby would never turn down an opportunity to tell a family story, but she needed to collect her thoughts. Her mind raced through the list of things she'd wanted to do during this visit: A half-dozen friends to see. Pearl and Harley's new house to inspect. Take the twins on a historical tour of the property. She was wondering how she was going to fit it all in, when she shouted, "I've got it! I know what we can do. Let's all get together at Camp Seminole, grill hamburgers and hot dogs and roast marshmallows over a fire. How about Friday evening?" Ruby anxiously looked around the room following her suggestion.

"I promised the Robertson's I'd babysit for them Friday night. They're celebrating their tenth wedding anniversary." Jewel was obviously disappointed that she'd made that commitment.

"Thurson and I both have a baseball game Friday evening, at seven o'clock," added Ralph.

Undeterred, Ruby then said. "Well, how about Saturday evening?"

There were several nodding heads and positive comments until Mr. Bill spoke up. "We can't, Pearl, we're supposed to take Matt and Laura out Saturday night, remember."

"Oh yeah, Ruby, I forgot to tell you, Matt Stamps is getting married, finally."

"No way!" exclaimed Ruby. "I thought that boy would be single forever. I had such a crush on him in high school, one of the football stars, big muscles, so cute. I just never could catch his eye, Lord knows I tried. Maybe it was the braces."

"More likely it was because there were so many girls chasing him that he just couldn't see all of them," corrected her sister. "His loss, I would say.

"Well, who's the lucky lady? Is she from around here?"

"From around here," exclaimed Mrs. Bill laughingly. "I'll say she is....do you remember Laura Livingston?"

"Laura...Laura Livingston," Ruby said softly while rubbing her chin. "I'm picturing a quiet girl, who always wore her hair in a pony tail, and her skirts halfway down to her ankles. And she was *forever* with her nose in a *book*." Ruby glared at her sister in disbelief. "*That, Laura Livingston?*"

"Apparently she got some fashion sense and some business sense to go along with the common sense she already had. And if you want to see what she looks like now, just check out the morning show on channel seven. She's the host. And on top of that, she's written two cookbooks and a travel guide to Nova Scotia."

For several seconds Ruby said nothing. She was processing this bit of information. This is not how she figured Laura Livingston would turn out. Now if her sister had told her that Laura had married a car salesman six months after graduating from high school, had four kids, and the largest collection of romance novels in the state; *that* would be the Laura Livingston she remembered.

"Bring them along," Ruby blurted out, "I mean, Matt's like a little brother to Harley. What better way to introduce his wife, to be, to the rest of the family. Besides you can take them out anytime."

"That sounds like a good idea," Gramps voiced his opinion. "I haven't seen that Matt Stamps in a year or more. How about it Harley, Pearl? You should bring them. And, Ralph, you should invite that young lady that you like, the one you were telling me about the other week."

Ralph's face turned bright red as he contemplated the unwanted attention that was sure to come. Dang it, he thought, now everybody knows; everybody would laugh at him. To his surprise, however, no one laughed, not even Fossendocker. Three or four family members did said they thought it was about time he realized there was something in this world besides sports. Fossendocker bit his lower lip and quietly took stock of the love-letter to Becky Boganthaul, safely stashed away in its hiding place. The letter that might not be as valuable as it once was, now that this was out in the open.

91

"All right," Mr. Bill finally said, "I suppose we could do that. Matt always enjoyed hanging around with all of us. I'm sure it would be fine with him."

"Great," said Ruby, "that settles it. Let's say six o'clock Saturday evening at Camp Seminole. I'll call the ladies around midweek to work out the menu.

Pleased with their plans and already looking forward to another family gathering, the Whitefox clan settled back to enjoy some lighthearted conversation before heading out for their respective homes.

***

"Hey dork, I heard you did a little ditch diving the other day." Ralph gave his little brother a sharp elbow to the ribs to go along with the teasing.

"Stop it, you big goon!" snapped Fossendocker as he repositioned his body so he could better protect his ribcage. "Don't talk to me, Ralph." He added in as stern a voice as he could muster up.

Mrs. Bill turned to glare at them from the front seat of the SUV. "I've had a wonderful day so far, and it's not your job to spoil that for me. So I don't want to hear another cross word out of either one of you. You do understand that, don't you?" Turning back to look out the windshield she mumbled. "You haven't seen each other in a week, it looks like you'd be glad to see each other again, but no...."

For the next several minutes the only sounds in the car were a vocal yawn from Mr. Bill, and the soft chatter from the third row seat, as Raelynn played with her baby doll.

"Hey Dad," said Fossendocker, as his dad turned onto Lamplighter Lane. "How many more days am I grounded? Hasn't it been a week already?"

"Almost son," his dad replied, "I figure a couple of more

evenings and you should have your debt paid off."

Ralph perked up right away, suddenly interested. What debt, he thought? Why is he grounded? "What have you done this time, Dock?" He had to ask, because curiosity was getting the best of him.

Fossendocker shot his big brother a hard stare, but before he could say anything his dad spoke up. He told Ralph about how Fossendocker had used the grease gun on his bike chain and ended up leaving the thing in the back yard. Mrs. Bill chimed in, telling how he had gotten grease on his new jeans, shoes, and socks. So there it went, Mr. and Mrs. Bill taking turns, telling every detail of the grease gun story, including the dishwasher. By the time they were finished, Ralph was laughing so hard that tears were rolling down his face.

Ralph was still laughing as they were getting out of their car and heading for the front door. "And all you got was grounded for a week, and having to work to pay for the stuff? Man, Dock you got off light. They should have sent you to boot camp." Ralph went straight to the telephone. "I've got to tell Thurson about this."

A few minutes later everyone could hear Ralph's laughter echoing through the house as he repeated the whole story to his cousin.

Fossendocker looked pleadingly at his dad, as if to say, come on Dad, make Ralph get off my case.

Instead his dad pulled him close in a big bear hug and said, "I wouldn't worry about it too much, son. Someday you'll laugh about it, too."

Maybe so, but right now he was pretty upset with everybody in the house except Raelynn. He headed for his bedroom and hopefully some privacy. Stretching out on the bed, he kicked off his shoes and stared at the ceiling. Soon his eyelids became heavy and his thoughts were as jumbled as a jigsaw puzzle in its box. A deep and restful slumber overcame the boy. He slept, he slept and dreamed of the white foxes of the Everglades.

BILL DALE GRIZZLE

CHAPTER 6

"I'm free, I'm free again." Fossendocker was happily singing his made-up song as he entered the kitchen. "No more restriction, I'm free again, I'm....going to ride my bike all day long, and sing my song. I'm free, I'm—"

"*No*, your not," his mother interrupted his vocals. "Remember falling into the ditch, remember being on the ramp, the ramp that your dad told you to stay off of? You were on that ramp because you chose to disobey your dad."

Fossendocker could not believe his ears. This *can't* be happening, he thought, I'm going to get grounded again. Oh no! Not again! His mind was reeling.

"Close your mouth, please, your sister might fall in" The scenario of his little sister falling into his wide open mouth may have been funny at some other time, but not right now. Mom was serious; her expression and tone of voice told him that much.

"But Mom, I *finished* my week. Dad said I did real good." There was no way to separate the grease gun thing, and the ditch thing, in his young mind. He was on restriction and anything he did during that time should be covered. Surely Mom could understand that. If she didn't, it sure wasn't because he wasn't explaining it in great detail.

During all this Mrs. Bill failed to notice that Raelynn had entered the kitchen and pulled one of the chairs over so she could climb up and peer into the birdcage.

"Come on Mom, this is not fair." Fossendocker was getting louder as he anxiously plead his case.

"Shhhhhh, your going to wake up Julio. He's still sleeping." Raelynn's words were barely above a whisper, but no matter, for the most part she was being ignored, anyway.

Mrs. Bill barely glanced in her direction. "Please don't fall off that chair." Then turned her attention back to her arguing son. "This *is* fair. And *this* is the way it's going to be." The volume of her voice was also up a few decibels. "I felt like you should get two more days restriction for disobeying your dad. That's serious you know. But Daddy said just one more day. He let you off light because you have been good for the past few days. He said that you've been very helpful and he's pleased with your interest in the new house."

"I won't ever get to ride bikes with Lenny again," the boy muttered, his chin resting on his chest in defeat.

"Of course you will, tomorrow. Anyway, he's visiting his grandparents and won't be home until tonight."

Fossendocker was shocked. His mom knows more about what his best friend is doing that he does.

"Here's the plan. I have the money you earned in my purse. We'll go by the hardware store so you can buy your dad a new grease gun, then to Coleman's for your jeans, and the grocery store for a bottle of cleaner. If there's any money left, it's yours to keep." Mrs. Bill studied the facial expression of her son, wondering what he was thinking. "Then you'll go with your dad this evening. There will be no pay this time. You'll help him because you love him, okay." Waiting for some kind of response from Fossendocker, who was certainly in a huff, her focus slowly shifted to what Raelynn was saying.

"I don't know how you can sleep with all the noise Mom and Dock are making." She was still speaking just above a whisper. "You must be real tired, Julio."

Turning around, Mrs. Bill could see her little girl still standing on the chair with her face almost touching the birdcage. "Better be careful, sweetie, that Julio might peck your nose."

"No, Mommy, he won't, Julio is sleeping," was the girl's quiet, yet confident reply.

"Does he have his head tucked under one of his wings?" Asked her mom. "They are so cute when they do that."

"No," Raelynn answered in a whisper, "he's just lying there, sound asleep."

With her mind still mostly on her exasperating, eleven-year-old boy it took a few seconds for Raelynn's reply to register. But when it did, she leapt from her chair and rushed to the birdcage. Sure enough there was Julio lying on his back, on the bottom of the birdcage, with his skinny little legs pointing straight up.

Mrs. Bill quickly sat Raelynn back onto the floor. "Dock, fix your sister a bowl of cereal, right now, please." When Raelynn's attention was on her breakfast, Mrs. Bill unlatched the cage door and cautiously reached inside. Julio did not respond to her touch, in fact poor Julio was as stiff as a fire poker.

"Oh, Julio," she whispered. The bird had been a part of the family for only a couple of years, but she and her little girl was fond of him, whether anyone else was or not. Actually, the Bill's were Julio's third family. Mrs. Bill brought him home one day after a friend talked her into keeping him while she was in Belize doing missionary work and teaching school. That lady, who was still in Belize, had gotten him from another lady who had married a gentleman who happened to be very allergic to birds.

"What a life," she continued to whisper to the recently

departed bird, "being stuck in a cage all the time....like being in prison, except you didn't do anything wrong." Movement caught her eye, and she turned to see Fossendocker standing no his tiptoes glaring into the birdcage.

Looking very dumbfounded and sounding even more so, he asked, "Mom is Julio....is he...."

"Yes, he's dead," was her whispered answer.

"What are you going to do with him, Mom?"

"I don't know. Wait until your daddy gets home I suppose. I guess your dad can bury him in the back yard."

"Hey, Mom, I know what we can do." Fossendocker replied enthusiastically. "We can take him to Gramps and let him burn some leaves and some of that smelly stuff that makes white smoke, and send his spirit back to the Great Father. You know like he did their old dog, Rusty."

Mrs. Bill just looked at her son. She'd been bound and determined to raise her children in a more traditional way of worship, breaking completely free from the ways of her own dad. But more and more she was realizing that the Whitefox heritage had a firm grip on this boy's spirit. She was also beginning to realize that this was not such a bad thing. So, nodding her head, she conceded.

"Fetch me a couple of those small white trash bags from the cabinet under the sink. Thank you. Now, please, help Raelynn pick out her cloths for the day, and then you get ready."

The kitchen was now free of children. Mrs. Bill gently placed Julio's little body into the first plastic bag, folded it inward, then rolled it up. She then placed that bag into a second bag and rolled it up tightly. Hurrying to the basement she put the plastic package into the freezer compartment of their spare refrigerator. *That should keep you until Saturday,* she thought, *then Gramps and Fossendocker can send you on your way.*

***

98

Stepping into Raddnick's Hardware Store was like stepping back in time. Compared to the modern day home improvement warehouses, which have been the demise of countless small-town hardware stores, this was not a huge place. But what it lacked in size it made up in character, and a most impressive inventory. The heart pine wooden floors moan and squeak the songs of time as customers walk across them. Yet they had supported shelves, racks and bins loaded with tons of nuts and bolts, tractor parts, shovels, chain saws, and thousands of other things, since Cleveland Raddnick had first opened the doors, more than eighty years before.

Gramps had once told Fossendocker that you could buy anything from a pot belly stove to a pot belly pig at Raddnick's. Looking around, he could believe it. There must be a million things in this place. The boy had no idea what most of this stuff was, or what it was for, but he sure would like to learn.

"What can I help you folks with today?" An older gentleman with silvery-white hair, whiskers and a pair of bushy eyebrows to match, approached them wearing a friendly smile.

Fossendocker studied the gentleman as he neared them. Not a hair on the top of his head, just a shinny dome, but plenty around the sides. That's weird, he thought. He knew enough about hair loss, from hearing his dad talk about it, to know this gentleman had not done this on purpose. But it sure looked like he could have.

Mrs. Bill nudged Fossendocker. That was his cue to tell the gentleman what he needed. "Yes sir, I need to buy a grease gun, please."

"Ah yes," said the man. He gave Mrs. Bill a quick wink and a nod to make her aware that Mr. Bill had let him know that they would be coming by. "Right this way young man." He led the boy to the section that held the grease guns, oil cans and the such. "Here you are. Is this going to be a gift for your daddy?"

"Well kind of.... I accidentally left his grease gun out in the yard and he ran over it with the lawnmower." Fossendocker was still looking around, there was just so much to look at in this store. "My Gramps says there's so much stuff in here that some things haven't been seen by human eyes in fifty years."

"Is that right?" Said the man with a chuckle. "Who is your Gramps, anyway?"

"Joseph Whitefox is my Gramps," the boy stated in such a manner that anyone hearing would have known he was proud of the fact.

"*Whitefox!*" He shouted. "I see that crazy ole Injun is still stirring up trouble."

The older gentleman's sparkling eyes and cheerful voice told the boy that he was kidding, and that he obviously knew his Gramps.

"You can tell that Gramps of yours that Dorsey Raddnick said that it didn't matter if there are a few things in this fine establishment that hasn't been seen in fifty years, I *still* know where they are."

Fossendocker nodded.

"Now if that's all you need, step right over here and I'll relieve you of some of your hard-earned money. But you're in luck today, young man, that grease gun is on sale. One dollar off the regular price."

Fossendocker followed Mr. Raddnick to the cash register and paid for the grease gun. He thanked him, and was about to rejoin his mom and little sister looking at the display of cowboy boots and hats, when the old gentleman stopped him with a hand on his shoulder.

Leaning over to get closer to the boy's ear he spoke in a quieter, more serious tone. "Get your Gramps to tell you about the time we scared the daylights out of the Tinsley sisters with that growling box his daddy made." Straightening up, he laughed. "But you can't tell anybody. We had half of Collie County out looking for the critter those girls swore was after them that night."

Again, Fossendocker nodded, but this time he managed a

semi-muted, "okay." A *growling box*. He had no idea what a growling box was but it sure sounded like something he needed to know about. The boy was already making plans to ask Gramps about it when he sees him on Saturday.

The next two stops were uneventful and, really, just down right boring. Thankfully, Fossendocker had all but completed his punishment. Just one more trip to the new house with his dad this evening. I wonder what he'll make me do today, he thought, as he stared out the window of his mom's car.

"How much money do you have left?" His mother's inquiry disrupted his thoughts.

"Two dollars and thirty-six cents," he answered, after retrieving it from his jeans pocket. Fossendocker stared at the two one dollar bills, a quarter, nickle, and six pennies for a few moments. "*All* that work and this is *all* I have left."

His mom let out an exaggerated laugh, causing the boy to wonder why she thought that was so funny.

"Do you have any idea how many times your dad and I have said that very same thing? Things have not always been like they are now, young fellow. When your daddy first started out it was a real struggle. We would look at what money was left over after the expenses were paid at the tire store and wonder how we would possibly have enough to pay the house payment, car payment, utilities, and still be able to buy food."

She quickly glanced at her son in the front seat beside her. Wow, she thought, I think he's actually listening. "And something else, we don't take anything for granted. Daddy and I remind each other from time to time how things used to be. So I truly hope that you've learned something from this experience."

"Sure Mom," he answered, "what's for lunch when we get home?"

"What a let down," Mrs. Bill mumbled, "a blue ribbon speech, and you want to know what's for lunch. I'm hurt, Dock."

"Sorry Mom. After lunch can I fill up the kiddie pool and

give Duke and Duchess a bath?"

"It's, *may I*, for the hundredth time. And that's a great idea, the dogs really need a good bath," said his mom. "Ralph should be finished with his yard work so he can help you. Then you two can wash my car."

Harley Bill pulled into the driveway behind his wife's car just as the two brothers were finishing the final rinse. Giving them a short blast of the horn he leaned out the window and said. "I would like a full service wash job, please."

Ralph shrugged and jokingly replied, "I don't know, sir, I can only do so much with the help I've got."

He and his dad got a laugh out of it, but Mr. Bill knew there was some seriousness to the matter.

"Work with him, son. Who knows, someday he may be your boss." Ralph cringed at that thought. "Just give it a quick rinse, to knock the dust off, before we go to the new house. The painters finished yesterday, and mom wants to inspect everything.

***

"Oh Harley, I just love it." Mrs. Bill stood in the middle of the living room turning in circles so she could see all of the space. "The color is perfect, it makes the room look huge. And the crown molding, I just love it, Harley. Come on, let's go look at the master bedroom."

That's when Fossendocker spotted it, the little black object on the window sill....a cell phone. He nonchalantly crossed the room and picked it up, wondering who it might belong to. Turning the phone over and over in his hand, he considered calling Leonard. He would pretend to be someone else, but then he remembered that his buddy wasn't at home, anyway. Better give this to Dad, he thought, and headed for his parent's new bedroom to catch up with the rest of his family. Just as he was approaching his dad with an outstretched hand, the cell phone rang. Well, not

102

exactly a ring, actually it was Latin style music. Of course this caught everyone by surprise, but Mr. Bill recovered quickly and took the phone from his son's hand. The caller ID identified the caller as Lena.

"Hello," he answered the call.

"Mester Bill," a heavily accented female voice, "is thees Mester Bill?"

"Yes, it is."

"Mester Bill, thees is Lena, wife of Carlos, the man who paints your new house. Carlos forget his cell phone today. Tomorrow he have job in Lincoln, is okay to come tomorrow, maybe six o'clock, get his phone?"

"Yes, yes that will be fine. Tell Carlos I'll take care of his phone, and I'll be here at the new house tomorrow. And tell him that Mrs. Bill is very happy with the painting, everything looks great."

They said their good byes, disconnected, and Mr. Bill put the phone in his pocket. From there it ended up on the kitchen counter at twenty-eight Lamplighter Lane, with instructions for Mrs. Bill to make sure it got back into his pocket for the return trip to the new house the following evening.

***

Mrs. Bill was watching her husband back out of the driveway, heading for work, when the telephone rang. Who could that be this early in the morning, she thought, as she hurried into the kitchen. Instantly she felt a little heart sick as she laid eyes on the empty birdcage. I forgot to tell Harley about Julio, how in the world could I have forgotten to tell him.

The poor lady of the house must have sounded distracted when she answered the phone, because the first thing Sadie Duvall said was, "Pearl, are you alright? You sound a little stressed."

Pearl Bill told her best friend the whole story about Julio,

103

from Raelynn thinking he was asleep to her depositing his little, white trash bag wrapped, carcass into the downstairs freezer. And then she added that somehow she had forgotten to tell Harley about it. She had just realized that fact as she was answering the phone.

"Wow, Pearl," there was a silence, "I'm so sorry." Two more seconds of silence, "Harley is really going to be upset with you for not telling him. You know how much he cared for that bird."

"Sadie, that was mean!" Mrs. Bill barked. "It's not funny, you know."

"I know it's not funny, Pearl, I was just trying to lighten matters up a little, because you sound so down."

"Well thanks for your efforts, I feel so much better now." Mrs. Bill added a little of her own sarcasm to the conversation. "Truth be known, the poor bird probably died from Harley Bill poisoning. He pecked a hole in the back of Harley's hand the other morning."

"Now that is funny," laughed Mrs. Duvall.

"I suppose it is," agreed Mrs. Bill. "By the way, why are you calling so early?"

"Oh yeah, my son is driving me crazy. He wanted me to call you to see if Dock is finished with his restriction. He's up and dressed and ready to hit the streets."

"How lucky for our neighborhood." A little more sarcasm from Mrs. Bill. "He's not up yet, his dad had him vacuum the whole house yesterday with that half worn out shop vacuum. He was so exhausted last night, I believe he was asleep before his head hit his pillow. But you can tell Lenny that he is off restriction. She could hear Leonard Lee celebrating in the background as his mom relayed the news.

"Here's some exciting news," Mrs. Bill continued. "The painters finished the house yesterday. Everything looks so good. Maybe we can ride over there later so you can see for yourself. If Rhonda's not busy, maybe she would like to spend a little time with Raelynn."

"Sounds great to me. Let's make it a lunch date. Rhonda is already up. Her daddy makes her get up before he leaves for work, but I can't talk to her for an hour or so, she's so ill. Her dad's trying to break her from staying up half the night and then wanting to sleep half the day....teenagers."

"Okay, call me back," said Mrs. Bill. She hung up the phone, poured a cup of coffee and treated herself to some hazelnut flavored coffee creamer. She turned on the TV in the living room just in time to see Laura Livingston introduce her next guest. She couldn't help but smile, remembering Ruby's reaction to the news that Matt Stamps was going to marry this lady in a little more than a week. "We'll ask Ruby to go to lunch with us," she said out loud. "This is going to be a good day."

Fossendocker wheeled his bicycle into the driveway just seconds behind his Aunt Ruby in her fire engine red rental car. He was to report home at eleven-thirty for additional instructions from his mom. It was only eleven-twenty-five, but there was no way he was going to jeopardize his precious freedom by being late.

"What's the hurry, Dock?" He breezed by his aunt with out saying a single word. "Well, good morning to you, too," she said, but he was already in the house.

Approaching the front door of her sister's house Ruby could see her young nephew practically standing at attention. His mother was really laying down the law. She concluded her lecture by making sure he understood that he and Leonard were not to wonder too far from home, check in with Rhonda every once in a while, and to not give her a hard time.

Considering his most recent predicament, the boy would gladly agree to anything she came up with. He just wanted to get back on that bicycle. "Okay, Mom. We'll be good, I promise."

"I made a half gallon of fruit punch; it's in the refrigerator. Get yourself a drink before you go back out." His mom playfully swatted him on the backside as he started for the kitchen, then turned her attention to her younger sister.

"Don't drink out of the jug, Dock, get a glass like a civilized person." He heard his mom call out just as his lips were about to make contact with the plastic container. Fossendocker took a deep breath, sighed and reached for a glass. How did she know that I was going to drink from the jug, he thought, and proceeded to pour a glass of fruit punch. Turning the glass up, the only reason he didn't drink the entire glassful was that he spotted the painter's cell phone lying on the cabinet. Instinctively he grabbed it and stuck it into his pocket. Then he finished his drink and rushed back through the living room and out the front door. He did, however, manage to mumble a hello to his aunt.

At the end of the driveway Leonard Lee Duvall was riding his bike in circles, impatiently waiting for his friend. "What took you so long, Dock? Did your mom make you take a nap?" Leonard thought this was funny; Fossendocker did not.

"Shut up, Lenny," he barked, "let's ride around the block, I have something good to show you."

"What," asked Leonard, "another love-letter?"

Fossendocker didn't answer, he just gave his buddy a sour look and rode off. Once they were out of sight of their houses, the two boys rolled to a stop under the shade of a big oak tree.

"So, Dock, what have you got this time?" Leonard asked.

Fossendocker produced the cell phone from his pocket. "This belongs to the painter, he left it at the new house. I was going to call you with it yesterday and play a trick on you, but you weren't home. But I got this other idea a few minutes ago. We're going to have some fun."

"Oh yeah," replied Leonard, "what are we going to do?"

"Mom said for us not to give Rhonda a hard time today while she's watching Raelynn. Well, that's no fun, we're supposed to give her a hard time. I mean that's our job, isn't it?"

Leonard nodded, "yeah."

"Well, you know how she runs to answer the phone every

time it rings, now," said Fossendocker.

"Ah, yeah, that's because some guy that likes her is calling all the time." My Dad said he's going to have a talk with him."

"Let's call your house, and when she answers, we'll hang up. We can see how many times it takes to make her real mad. If Ralph hadn't gone to the tire shop with Dad today, we would do it to him, too."

Leonard was grinning from ear to ear. "Boy, that's really going to make her mad. Let's see, we could sit in the living room. That way she would go to the kitchen phone. I got it Dock, we can pretend we're reading comic books. That way we can hide the cell phone, and we can see what she's doing, and when we laugh she'll think we're laughing at the comic books."

"That's it, Lenny! What a plan! Let's make sure our moms are gone." Fossendocker was already laughing at their scheme.

Safely hidden in Leonard's bedroom the boys picked out a few comic books, figured out how to disable the cell phone's ringer and turn off any other audible sounds it might make. Then they finalized their plans, knowing full well the trouble they would be in should they get caught.

Both boys took up their positions, Fossendocker on one side of the living room would operate the cell phone. Leonard sat where he could see into the kitchen; he would give Fossendocker a signal when Rhonda was about to pick up the kitchen phone. They could plainly hear Raelynn chattering away in Rhonda's bedroom. Everything was all set.

Fossendocker dialed the Duvall's home number and pressed the send button. Two or three seconds later the telephone rang. Just as planned Rhonda ran from her room, through the living room, and into the kitchen. Leonard gave the signal and Fossendocker pressed the end button just as she was reaching for the phone. All Rhonda heard was a dial tone. She hung up the phone and returned to her room. Three minutes later she was running through the house to answer the phone again. This time

107

she muttered something that neither boy understood. This brought on even more laughter from the boys, who had their faces buried in comic books.

The third time, she verbally assaulted the phone and slammed down the receiver *very* hard. On the return trip to her bedroom she glared at the two laughing boys. Her eyes were burning with anger, her lips formed a tight straight line. Although, she had no idea the two boys were laughing at her, the simple fact that they *were* laughing made her life just a little more miserable. *"Why aren't you two creeps outside, anyway?"* She yelled hatefully, then stomped off.

They pretended not to notice her, or hear her rude comment, but as soon as she was out of sight they both looked over their comic books at each other. Leonard held up one finger and mouthed, one more time. Later, as they laughed about their stunt, they'd both felt like it might have been a little risky, but, Fossendocker had nodded back and pressed the send button. For the fourth time Rhonda headed for the kitchen, but this time she didn't run. Now she was angry. Once again, hearing nothing but the dial tone, she *totally lost* it. Viciously hammering the counter top with the telephone receiver, Rhonda screamed a mouthful of choice phrases, including a long string of curse words.

Leonard and Fossendocker could not believe what they were hearing. Some of the things that came out of Rhonda's mouth were foreign to their ears. This had to be one of their better stunts, maybe even their very best, but still, cursing was not allowed at either of their homes, period.

"*I heard that,*" yelled Leonard, "you just wait till I tell Dad what you said."

Rhonda darted into the room, stopped in front of Leonard Lee and placed her hands on her hips. "You are not going to tell Dad *anything*, you rotten little weasel."

Fossendocker could see that Rhonda's fists were clinched so tight that her knuckles had turned white. She towered over her brother and he feared for his friend. So he took this opportunity to slip the cell phone back into his pocket, toss his comic book onto the coffee table, and head for the front door. If his best friend was going to get his tail kicked by his sister, he did not want to see it. Once outside, however, he could still hear the heated exchange.

"Oh yeah, I'm going to tell him, you trash mouth." Leonard was now standing up to his, seven inches taller, older sister and holding his own. "And I'm going to tell him how you beat the cabinet with the phone. Boy, you've had it, Rhonda, you've really had it this time. Dad won't let you see that guy, what's his name, Snot, ever again. And you'll be grounded for a change, instead of me." Leonard slid past Rhonda and started for the front door.

"*It's Scott,*" she screamed at him, "his name is Scott. *Idiot!*" The extremely angry sixteen-year-old girl grabbed a comic book from the coffee table and hurled it across the room at her little brother's back. Of course it fluttered harmlessly to the floor, like a baby bird's failed first attempt at flight. Just short of the front door Leonard turned around and, for a few seconds, both he and Rhonda stared at the comic book on the floor. And then their eyes met. For a full ten seconds they glared at each other before Leonard continued out the door, shaking his head, as if in utter disbelief.

An alarmed looking Raelynn stuck her head past a corner to investigate the commotion just in time to see Rhonda throw herself into the nearest chair. "Are you okay, Rhonda?" She asked, as she cautiously approached the teenaged girl.

The vision of her kid brother staring at the comic book in the floor, then walking out the front door shaking his head without saying anything else, was stuck in her mind. His coolness and composure in that moment had stifled her anger and instantly she could think more clearly. The blank look on Rhonda's face told Raelynn that she was not okay.

"I have really done it this time." she muttered, still staring at the opposite side of the room. "I have broken almost every number one rule of the Duvall house at the same time. Lenny's right, Dad's going to ground me," her gaze shifted to Raelynn, "forever."

Paul Duvall was not even close to being the tyrant his children thought him to be. He was simply a no-nonsense dad, and he had a lot of number one rules of the Duvall house: No cussing, no name calling, no yelling at your parents, no slamming doors, no throwing things, no outburst of anger, and so on. One who was not his child might actually find humor in this. How could they *all* be the number one rule? Once when Rhonda was thirteen and was in the process of being scolded for a number one rule infraction, she questioned her Dad about how the number one rule always seemed to change. Well you guessed it, the number one rule of the Duvall house was then, *never* question the number one rule system.

Consoling her friend, Raelynn wrapped her arms tightly around the perplexed teenager, "it'll be okay," she softly said.

Poor Rhonda had absolutely no idea how badly she had been set up by the two rascals, who had just peddled their bicycles back to the Bill house. They were at that moment rolling in the grass laughing hysterically.

"Lenny, are you really going to tell on Rhonda?" Fossendocker finally managed to ask his best friend.

"Shoot no!" exclaimed Leonard Lee, still laughing, "it will be a lot more fun watching her worry about it."

"Ah, man that's so funny, Lenny," laughed Fossendocker. "You did real good in there, I thought she was going to clobber you. I've never seen her so mad."

Leonard just nodded, unable to speak through his howling laughter.

"Come on, let's put this cell phone back in the kitchen before Mom gets back," said Fossendocker. "We sure don't want to get caught with it. They might think we've been up to something." And that brought on another laughing fit.

With the cell phone safely back on the kitchen counter, the Lamplighter Legends were once again on the ride. Cruising the streets of Olde Towne, they would stop occasionally to converse with a friend or to talk about the prank they had played on Rhonda. Fossendocker told Leonard about the family cookout planned for Saturday at Camp Seminole and asked if he would like to go.

"Sure, I would," exclaimed Leonard, "if Mom and Dad will let me."

"You could spend the night. I think Ralph is going to invite his," Fossendocker made a really nasty-sounding gagging noise, "girlfriend. My Aunt Ruby is going to tell a family story, too"

"What's that," inquired Leonard, "what's a family story?"

Fossendocker explained to his buddy about how the stories had been passed down from one generation to the next, all committed to memory.

"You mean all that junk is true?" Leonard asked, looking a little skeptical.

"It's not junk," corrected Fossendocker. "And yes, it's all true. It's the history of my people."

"Your people? You are for sure not an Indian." Leonard looked at his best friend with his eyes drawn close together in doubt.

"I may not look like an Indian," replied Fossendocker with authority, "but my Gramps says that on the inside, I'm all Seminole. Hey, we better head back to your house. Mom said for us to check in with Rhonda every now and then."

"Hey Dock, when we get back to my house let's act like nothing happened earlier. That'll really mess with her head."

"Great idea, Lenny. Let's go!"

The boys made one more loop around the block and then checked in with Rhonda. Of course, Rhonda, was still in a terrible state, and could not have cared less that the boys were following their mother's instructions.

***

For the next several days things were very cool between Rhonda and her younger brother. In fact she could hardly look him in the eyes, feeling certain that he would spill the beans any second. Finally, after almost a week, Leonard Lee approached his sister with the idea of a truce.

Rhonda listened intently as Leonard read over each stipulation of the treaty. "In exchange for my silence you agree to these terms: You will never tell on me for anything I do, no matter how rotten. You will not yell at me and call me names, especially weasel. You will share your snacks and soft drinks with me. You will let me watch what I want to on TV. And when you get your drivers license you will take me where I want to go, when I want to go."

I don't know which is worse, she thought, being grounded for five years or being blackmailed by your kid brother. He really is a weasel. She was surely studying the face of a future politician. That smirky little smile....I'll be glad when he gets his braces, that'll fix that silly grin. And maybe he'll catch the worst case of acne in history.

"*Nah, nah,*" she was shaking her finger at him before she could stop herself, "you didn't come up with all this garbage by yourself. You're not even smart enough to come up with something like this. That Dock put you up to it, didn't he, and he wrote that list, didn't he?"

"Did not!" Leonard yelled. "You think Dock's the only smart guy around here? You gonna sign this or not?"

They sat in silence for several seconds. "You know, Mom's been wondering why the kitchen phone's not working right." Leonard quietly said.

With that, Rhonda felt panic welling up in her chest. She grabbed the pen and signed her name on the treaty. "*Get out of my room,*" her voice was harsh and hateful, "*get out of my room, and don't ever come in here again, you little—*"

Leonard held up his hand to stop her in mid-sentence, and

tapped the paper she had just signed, with his forefinger. Still wearing his smirky little smile he folded the notebook paper, crammed it into his back pocket, and left his sister's bedroom. For once in his life Leonard felt like he had the upper-hand. He was really going to enjoy this.

BILL DALE GRIZZLE

CHAPTER 7

S aturday morning dawned with partially overcast skies, on and off drizzle, and the possibility of a quickly moving thunder shower or two. Gramps stood on the front porch of his home looking down at the horseshoe bend in Brightwell Creek. How he loved this place, and often spent long periods of time reminiscing about his life on this land. His father had worked hard all his life to provide for his wife and children, and his mother had been, quiet simply, a wonderful mother. His love and respect for them would never fade. He should only hope that his own children would feel the same way about him and Grams when they no longer walked upon this earth. His thoughts turned to his gratefulness and how the Great Father had always provided them with much more than they really needed. Why, he was even grateful for the rain that would force him to reschedule the fishing trip with Fossendocker to Pig's Eye Lake.

A bright flash of lightening followed very closely by the roar of thunder brought him quickly back to the present. Gramps was heading for the front door when he heard Ruby call out to him.

"Daddy are you ready for another cup of coffee, or are you just going to stand out there and get struck by lightening." That was, of course, Ruby's way of encouraging him to come inside.

"I have never been struck by lightening before," he was saying as he walked into the kitchen where Grams and Ruby were having coffee. "But we did have a cow one time that got struck. Killed her graveyard dead, didn't it, Grams?"

"It sure did," agreed Grams, nodding. "We hadn't been married but about six months and I still wasn't quiet used to living so far out in the country, so it scared the stuffing out of me. Lightening struck that big pine tree, and that poor cow happened to be standing in the wrong place at the wrong time."

"You've never mentioned that before." Ruby looked puzzled, first at her mom, then her dad.

"I guess that's just one of those things that got stuck way back somewhere in the gray matter," he replied, then shrugged his shoulders. "I'd better call Dock to let him know we won't be going fishing this morning."

"Would you like some breakfast?" asked Grams.

During his call to his grandson she sat a bowl of oat meal on the kitchen table in front of him. Gramps stared at it for a few seconds before looking up at his wife. "I reckon we're out of bacon and eggs," he mumbled.

Grams placed her hands flat on the table, leaned over until she was only inches from her husband's face. "As far as you're concerned, we are. You don't need the cholesterol."

"Even if it wasn't raining I couldn't go fishing today, Dock, I'm too weak from hunger. But at least the weatherman said these rain showers would be out of the area by mid-day. The weather should be about perfect for our cookout this evening." Gramps and Dock chatted for a few more minutes, with Gramps telling him that it was great that his friend Lenny was coming to the cookout with him. And Fossendocker reminded his grandfather that he needed to send Julio's spirit on its way.

116

Ruby's twin daughters scampered into the kitchen just as Gramps was saying good bye to Fossendocker. They were both scrambling to sit on his knee, somehow they both managed to get into his lap. "I wish you two didn't have to go home tomorrow," he said, "why don't you stay for a while longer and then Grams and I can put you in a big box and send you home in the mail, right before school starts back."

Faith and Henna giggled at this suggestion as they both studied the face of the grandfather they only got to see two or three times a year.

"How about their other granddaddy?" Gramps was admiring the twins, but directed the question to Ruby.

"They call him Grandy and she is Toppy. Grandy is almost as big of a nut as you are, Daddy. And Toppy spoils them rotten. They are wonderful grandparents."

"Oh, we know all that, we talk to them every three of four months." Gramps said this with a twinkle in his eyes. "I meant, how's his health, he was having some blood pressure problems, wasn't he?"

Ruby glared at her dad, then at her mom. Would her family ever stop surprising her? She had absolutely no idea that her parents had had any contact at all with Thomas' parents after their wedding. Her in-laws certainly had never mentioned it.

I'm *not* going to let him know that surprised me so much, she thought. "Oh, he's doing fine now, finally got his blood pressure regulated, and they've got him on a better diet. He's even lost several pounds." Ruby again looked at her mom, who was smiling behind her coffee cup. "You two....."

***

Harley Bill, Fossendocker, and Leonard Lee pulled into Camp Seminole to find Gramps cleaning the grill with a wire brush. "For once that weatherman was right," he called out as the boys were scrambling from the pickup truck. "Turned out to be a beautiful day. There's even a little nip in the air, shouldn't be too hot for a small fire to roast those marshmallows."

Gramps extended his hand towards Leonard. "Haven't seen you in a long time there, L.L., how in the world have you been?"

"Doing fine, Gramps." Leonard took the hand of the man he actually admired even more than his real grandfather. He had even, on occasion, shared with his best friend that he wished Gramps really was his grandfather.

Gramps greeted his eleven-year-old grandson with the same kind of handshake, then reached for his approaching son-in-law's hand but hesitated when he saw the bandage.

"What's up with that?" asked Gramps, noting that a week ago it was a simple band-aid.

"That blasted bird," Mr. Bill frowned at the same time he pointed at the little white package that his son held. "It's infected where that little monster pecked me. I had to go to the doctor yesterday for some antibiotics. You know, old Doc Hanley is about a basket case. He said I had bird peck fever."

"Why, I never heard of such malarkey!" shouted Gramps, laughing at his son-in-law. "Explain to me what that is."

"Yeah, that's what he said alright, bird peck fever," continued Mr. Bill. "Apparently it's a really rare medical condition caused by a bird peck, followed by repeated exposure to oil, grease, and road dirt from car tires."

Gramps was howling at his son-in-law. "Yep, old Doc Hanley is something else alright. One time I went to him 'cause I had a big splinter in my finger that I couldn't get out. He got it out all right, but on the insurance form he put down that he had to perform a *lumber-ectomy*. I guess he thought that was funny. The insurance company didn't, though, and he never did get his money from the them. I ran into him and his wife one day at Miss Millie's and he told me about it. I tried to pay him but he wouldn't hear of it. So I bought their lunch and suggested to him that he stop trying to be a comedian. I figured we were even. Lunch and a good piece of advice. That goes a long way, right?"

"I'd say so, too. By the way, there's that bird." Mr. Bill once again pointed to the bundle that Fossendocker held. "Good riddance to that squawking creature. Gramps, you and the boys are welcome to do your funeral thing. I really hate it for Pearl and Raelynn that he up and died, but I for one, *will not* miss him. I brought a shovel, too."

Gramps chuckled at his son-in-law, and how Julio had gotten the best of him. "Yeah, we had better do that before all the girls get here. Those little girls might think it's gross." Gramps made a face, mocking his little granddaughters, then turned to his grandson, who was inching his way toward the creek. "Hey, Dock, let's build a small fire over at the edge of the clearing and send this old bird on his way. Come sit with us at the fire, L.L."

Leonard was thrilled at the prospect of taking part in a real Native American ceremony. He and Fossendocker hustled over to Gramps' truck where he was gathering up an arm load of wood.

"Got some rich pine kindling here," said Gramps. "It burns real good and it's easy to start a fire with kindling like this. Let's put most of it by the fire pit but we'll carry a few sticks with us." He loaded each boy with sticks of wood, who were then so preoccupied by their loads that they didn't notice Gramps retrieving a leather bag from the cab of his truck.

"What's in the bag, Gramps?" Fossendocker finally asked as his grandfather placed the bag on the ground at the spot where they would build a small ceremonial fire.

"You'll see in a minute," he responded, "first let's pick a place to plant this old bird."

"How about right here?" They had walked about fifty feet into the woods. "Here's a nice dogwood tree that Julio's spirit can soar up into. Let's take him out of that bag, the earth doesn't need that plastic and neither does Julio." In the process of removing the bird, Gramps plucked a feather from each of Julio's wings.

119

Fossendocker and Leonard both agreed that this would be a fine spot, and after a few scoops with the shovel in the soft, rich soil, the late Julio was laid to rest.

"Each piece of wood represents something, my sons. This one represents mankind, this one, the bird. Their paths crossed and the lives of mankind were effected. Why, if not for this crossing," Gramps placed the two sticks into the makeshift fire ring they'd created with a half dozen stones, forming an X, "your dad wouldn't have bird peck fever." Gramps pointed another stick in Fossendocker's direction, and then another in Leonard's, nodding his head with authority. "These two sticks represent you two, and this one me. These are the branches of the dogwood that stands guard over Julio's resting place. This final piece of wood represents the Great Father, from which all things come, and all things must return." All these pieces of wood were carefully placed into the fire ring.

At this point the two boys watched in awe as Gramps pulled a long leather shirt from the bag, stood and slipped it on. It hung to mid-thigh, with leather lacing, and was decorated with various kinds of beads and buttons made from sea shells.

"This deerskin shirt was made by the oldest daughter of Micco Sando Whitefox," said Gramps as he returned to the ground and placed a bright red sash over his left shoulder. This, too, was decorated with beads and buttons made from shells.

Fossendocker was speechless. He could not believe that he had never seen these items. But it was the third thing from the bag that caused his mouth to drop open. A turban-style headdress, the same bright red as the sash, decorated with a band of black and a band of gold and embellished with several carefully placed shells. On the right side of the headdress were two eagle feathers, one pointing to the front, the other almost straight up. Hanging from the left side of the headdress was a fox tail. But not just any fox tail, this one was brilliant white.

"Wow, Gramps." Both boys reached over to touch the soft

120

white fur. "Wow, Gramps," Fossendocker repeated, almost in a whisper. "Is it real?"

"Yes, Dock, it's real alright, as a matter of fact this is the tail from the very first white fox that Micco Sando spotted, the one that he released from his trap."

The two boys continued to gently stroke the soft, white fur. "I can't believe somebody killed her," said Fossendocker. His voice was husky and sorrowful.

"Oh no!" exclaimed Gramps. "She wasn't killed, not by a person anyway. The white foxes were protected by *all* the People. If someone had killed her, they would have surely been fed to the alligators. Three summers after Micco Sando discovered the existence of the white foxes, a great storm struck all of south Florida. There was much flooding and winds that blew many trees to the ground. Stories have it that more than a dozen of our People were lost to this storm." Gramps lowered his voice and reached up to his shoulder to place his hand on the white fur. "She was also a victim of the mighty winds. The day after the rains stopped, a good and loyal friend of Micco Sando discovered her body while he was checking his traps. A really large limb had broken from a grand old oak tree and crushed her. The only part of her that could be seen was her tail. You see, boys, she was halfway into her den."

Fossendocker's eyes were as big as silver dollars and Leonard's mouth was hanging open in disbelief. "That's terrible!" Fossendocker finally yelled.

Gramps smiled his big toothy smile. "So it may seem, but the Great Father always has a way with his creatures. It turned out that she had three pups in that den. Two of them were white. If she'd made it into the den they all would have been trapped by that big limb. Had she not made it halfway into the den, the pups would have been trapped. She would not have been able to rescue them, nor would they have ever been found. So you see the Great Father took her in order to save her pups. The three pups and the body of the mother white fox were brought to the People where the pups were nursed to an age that they could be returned to the wild. And mother white fox, as she had become known, was given a proper send off."

Fossendocker had never heard a word of this before now and was completely caught by surprise. Searching for something to say, he pointed at the tail that hung gracefully from the headdress and rested upon the left shoulder of the grandfather that always seemed to be full of surprises.

For a few moments Fossendocker searched the face of his grandfather; it almost felt like he had gone back in history a hundred years, or more. If not for his sparkling green eyes, no one would ever suspect that he was anything but one hundred percent Native American. Add the deerskin shirt, the sash, and the headdress, and Fossendocker could only smile at what he saw. Not only was he looking at a man that *could* have been the leader of the People, he was indeed looking at the man that *is* the leader of *his* People.

Gramps continued his story. "At first the tail was used to comfort her orphaned pups. After they were returned to the wild, this tail, these two feathers, these shells, and these bones were taken to an old woman in the village. She was known through out all the villages as the greatest of headdress makers. Following instructions from the leader of the People, a sash and headdress was fashioned....a sash and headdress like none other before it, or after it. They were given to Micco Sando Whitefox at the birth of his first child, and were proclaimed to be forever worn only by a member of the Whitefox Clan." Gramps gazed at the pair of silent lads. "What do you think about me telling the whole story someday?"

Still speechless, the two boys could only nod as they continued to stare at Gramps who had returned to the task of preparing the fire. Tucking a fist full of dried moss underneath the rich pine sticks, he removed a piece of metal, not unlike a dull knife blade, and a chunk of flint from the bag.

122

Sparks flew from the flint, and into the dried moss, as he struck the stone with the metal. After three or four attempts he tossed these tools aside. "These things work better nowadays," he grumbled and then pulled a box of matches from his pants pocket.

This got a reaction from Fossendocker and his friend, they both giggled and Leonard quietly said, "alright, Gramps."

With the fire crackling away, Gramps placed the feathers from Julio's wings into the flame. "Fly safely great bird, and may your beak be as effective on all your enemies as it was on Harley Bill's hand."

This brought another giggle from the boys.

Gramps smiled at the two sniggering boys and began his chant. "HaaaaaYaaaa, HaaYaaaaa, HoooooOYa, HiYaaaaa, HiYaaa, HaaHaaYooooooooo....."

In the midst of all this chanting, Gramps tossed a pinch of black gunpowder into the fire causing a small poof and a little cloud of smoke. Continuing his chant, he waved his arms from one side, of the now much smaller fire, to the other. Finally extending his hands out over the tiny bed of red and orange glowing coals, Gramps declared. "It is done."

"Wow, Gramps," Fossendocker was very excited, "I didn't know you could speak Seminole. Can you teach me how to speak Seminole, can you?"

Gramps slapped his knee, laughing out loud. "Shoot Dock," he flatly stated, "that wasn't Seminole, that was something I got off the television. Sounds pretty good though, don't it."

Not expecting that at all, the two boys simply stared at Gramps for a few seconds before bursting into laughter and rolling backwards on the still slightly damp grass.

"Your Gramps is out of control," snorted Leonard.

Fossendocker could only nod in agreement, as he caught a glimpse of Gramps repacking his bag.

With all the send-off ceremony excitement the two boys had failed to notice that most of the other family members and their guest had arrived at Camp Seminole.

"Let's head back and join the others," said Gramps, "before they think we're up to something."

Matt Stamps was introducing his fiancee to everyone as Gramps and the two boys approached. Gramps gave Matt a hardy handshake and a gentlemanly slap on the back before greeting Laura Livingston.

"I have always considered Matt to be part of my son-in-law's family. Therefore he is part of my family, as you will be, too. We welcome you, and congratulate you both. My name is Joseph Whitefox, everybody here calls me Gramps." He released his gentle hold on her right hand and pointed in the direction of his wife, who had busied herself with the food preparations. "And that ole woman is called, Grams."

Grams shook the serving spoon she was holding at Gramps but refrained from saying anything, at least for the time being.

Laura looked over at Grams, smiled and gave her a little wave, although they had already been introduced. She quickly looked back at Gramps. What a fascinating man, she thought, as her TV show host skills were kicking in. He's obviously Native American, but what about those green eyes. And I wonder what they were doing over there at the edge of the woods.

"Mr. Whitefox, I am—" She stopped in mid-sentence as Gramps held up his hand and mouthed "Gramps." She started over, "Gramps, I am honored to be here with your family."

Ruby stepped up beside Laura. "By the way, J.D. called a few minutes ago. He said they're running a little behind schedule. Thurson dropped the tea again. Can you believe that?"

Gramps shook his head. "Probably had his mind on last night's ball game. They lost by one run, only their second loss of the season."

"That's too bad," replied Ruby. "But I'm going to steal this girl away from you." She grabbed Laura by the hand, pulling her toward the creek and away from the others. "We haven't seen each other since high school and we've got some catching up to do."

J.D. and his family finally arrived with a new container of tea. Thurson found himself on the receiving end of a little ribbing for having dropped the tea for the second time in a week. His dad let everyone know that he thought it strange that wild horses couldn't pull a baseball out of Thurson's hands, but he couldn't seem to be able to hold on to a tea jug, with a handle. Everyone laughed and chattered, and all was well at Camp Seminole......for about half an hour.

Fossendocker was slowly and deliberately chewing a bite of hot dog, as he studied the face of his older brother. Gross, he thought, as he watched Ralph make googly eyes at Becky Boganthaul.

Leonard's poke in the side brought Fossendocker back to the moment. "They're holding hands," Leonard was whispering, "they're holding hands, Dock."

"I know, this is a lot more serious than I thought." Fossendocker whispered back to Leonard as their eyes met. "They're really grossing me out."

Suddenly everyone's ears were filled with the high-pitched roar of some kind of machine, and the noise was getting louder. Then, to the great surprise of all, a motorcycle burst into the clearing, heading straight toward them.

"What the—" exclaimed J.D. as the dirt bike made two complete circles around the picnic shelter, making plenty of noise and throwing up a trail of grass and dirt.

Gramps came to his feet, waving his arms in an attempt to get the long-haired boy, with no helmet, to leave, which he did after his second lap.

The obnoxious sound of the dirt-bike faded as quickly as it had come, leaving everyone wondering the same thing. Who in the world was that?

Gramps answered that question. "That was Dub Dillard's boy. Dub just lets him run wild. He needs that motorbike like I need a battleship." Gramps returned to his meal and in about thirty seconds everything was back to normal.

"Hey everybody, Aunt Ruby is almost ready to begin her story," called out Jewel. She had been looking forward to this all week, so she was the first person to grab a seat at the fire pit, right beside her Aunt Ruby. Others scrambled for their places. Naturally Fossendocker ended up on one side of Gramps, Leonard on the other.

"What's this all about?" Laura whispered to Matt as they settled into the folding bag chairs they'd brought.

"Oh, you're in for a real treat," replied Matt. "I've only heard Ruby tell a story once, years ago, but I've heard Gramps tell stories a number of times."

Laura gave Matt a puzzled look. He hadn't quiet answered her question. She shrugged, signaling him for more information.

"The Whitefox Family has scores of stories, all committed to memory, that they recall from time to time. Some are long and full of details, others are shorter, but they are all a piece of their history. They teach their children about their ancestors, and through these stories there is a bond that you and I will never fully understand."

Laura only nodded, but Matt recognized that look. "No, no, forget it Laura. This is too personal, Gramps would never go for it."

Laura smiled and patted Matt on the knee. "Well you can't blame me for thinking about it; it would make an interesting show." I'll talk to Ruby later, she thought, then settled back sipping her iced tea.

Waiting as patiently as he could for the story to begin, Fossendocker looked around for his older brother. There he was, down by the creek, still hanging on to Becky Boganthaul's hand, smiling like it was his birthday or something. He was so lost in thought about how Ralph was all in love, that he almost missed the beginning of the story.

126

"In the white man's year 1832 many of the Creek were driven from their homelands and expelled to lands west of the Mississippi River. Within four or five years almost all had been removed from their homes. Only a few managed to avoid being forced off their lands by hiding out and moving around from place to place." Ruby took a deep breath as she paused for a few seconds. "This was the darkest and most painful time in the history of our People. They became victims of cruelty, famine, disease, and death. But the one thing the People refused to become a victim of, was hopelessness. And through their hope, regardless of how dim it must have been, a way was made for there to be born, a girl. A girl who came to be named Virginia LaFeaull. She was my Father's mother."

Everyone situated around the fire pit was mesmerized by Ruby's story, as she spun chapter after chapter about how Grandmother Virginia's mother, a young Creek maiden, had moved to New Orleans to find employment. She had found work as a housekeeper in the home of a wealthy businessman, and through this position she'd met a young Frenchman named Claude LaFeaull. Captain Claude LaFeaull had gotten his hands on an old, but sea worthy vessel and had established a shipping route between New Orleans and Galveston. The handsome young Frenchman and the lovely Creek maiden, known only as Flee, fell in love, and were married in the year 1916.

Ruby paused once more, took a sip of water, looked around the fire pit, catching the eye of each person gathered to hear her story. Gramps had instilled in her that to be a successful story teller, you must have listeners. Therefore he had taught her a few subtle tricks to help maintain the attention of the audience. His twinkling eyes and slight nod told her that she was doing very well.

"All was well with the happy couple, and in the year 1918 their first and only child was born. She was named Virginia, after the wife of the wealthy businessman that Flee had worked for.

Even though, Lady Virginia, as she was called, was from a rich family and held high social ranking, it had not spoiled her heart. She befriended Flee and loved her as if she were her sister."

"Now, the ambitious Captain LaFeaull fully intended to provide well for his beloved wife and daughter so he added a second vessel to his shipping line. He was well on his way to becoming financially independent. However, tragedy struck when Virginia was only four years old. Within sight of the coast of Texas a hurricane sank her father's ship, taking with it eleven of the fourteen men aboard. Somehow three men survived and all relayed stories of Captain LaFeaull's gallant efforts to save his men and his ship. When the news of the fate of her husband was delivered to Flee she fainted from the shock and toppled down the front steps of their house. Poor Flee was severely injured in the fall, and although Lady Virginia tended to her with the best medical care available, broken ribs and a broken heart were more than she could recover from. Flee contracted pneumonia and in the span of less than five weeks young Virginia LaFeaull lost both her father and her mother."

Laura Livingston caught hold of Matt's forearm with a strong grip. "Is this for real?" She asked him in a very quiet voice, as to not disturb the story. "That's one of the saddest things I've ever heard."

Matt simply patted her hand and nodded.

After taking another sip of water, Ruby was once again weaving her way through her grandmother's life; reassuring her listeners that the tragedies that young Virginia experienced did not follow her all her days. The Lady Virginia raised her as her own daughter. She was well educated, well traveled, and experienced many things that most young ladies of her time, especially young Native American ladies, did not.

After forty minutes Ruby concluded her story with a touching account of how George William Whitefox and Virginia LaFeaull met in a restaurant, just off the campus of Jefferson

University, where she was in her third year of college education. She was smitten by the handsome young Seminole, and with one smile his heart was hers. Virginia finished her education and they were married in 1940. George and Virginia enjoyed almost fifty years together, raised two children, and had seven grandchildren. But that is getting into another story for another time.

As was customary, the Whitefox Clan nodded their heads and quietly voiced their approval and appreciation of the story.

Finally Laura could stand it no longer and blurted out. "Ruby Whitefox, that has to be one of the most fascinating things I've ever heard in my life. You should write a book." Others agreed, but what Laura was really thinking was, you should write a book, then come on my show to introduce it to the world.

"I'm flattered," said Ruby.

"I'm serious," Laura bluntly stated, "we should exchange numbers and I'll have my agent contact you."

Ruby, feeling a little embarrassed, opened her mouth to object, but nothing came out. She simply smiled and nodded.

By that time the place was once again buzzing with chatter and laughter. Gramps stood up, stretched, and began making his way toward the picnic shelter. By the time Fossendocker caught up with him he had a pair of chocolate chip cookies in his grasp.

"Gramps, I need to ask you something." The boy wanted to take advantage of their time alone.

"Sure thing, Dock, what's on your mind?" Replied his grandfather, offering him one of the cookies, which he declined.

"Mr. Raddnick at the hardware store told me to ask you about the time you two scared those girls with a growling box that your daddy made, but he told me to keep it a secret."

Gramps sat down on one of the picnic table benches, rubbing his chin as if he were in deep thought. "Raddnick, huh, that ole coot is going to get us both in trouble yet, wagging that tongue of his. How much did he tell you about that incident?"

"That's about all Gramps." The boy searched his memory.

"Oh yeah, he called you an *Injun* and said you're still stirring up trouble. And it didn't matter what you said about all his stuff in his store, he knows where everything is."

Just as Gramps was explaining that it might be time for him to go by the hardware store and take that old fellow down a notch or two, Leonard walked up.

Great, thought Fossendocker, now I won't get to hear about the growling box. Gramps read that look on his grandson's face very well.

"Dock," Gramps sounded pretty solemn, "do you think L.L. can be trusted to know about the growling box?"

"Sure he can Gramps, he's my best buddy and we have a pact. We know all of each others secrets."

Leonard was nodding. "I can be trusted." He had no idea what they were talking about, but it sounded serious and he wanted to be a part of it.

"Okay then," Gramps continued, "I'll pick you two up about eight o'clock Monday morning. First we'll go by the hardware store and I'll give that Dorsey Raddnick a lickin'. Then we'll head over to Pig's Eye and catch some of those big ole bream before they quit biting. L.L., I'll call your mama and daddy and make it all right. And don't worry about a fishing pole and tackle, I've got all that covered."

"But Gramps," Fossendocker protested, "what about the growling box?"

"Don't you worry about that till Monday. Dorsey Raddnick opened this can of worms, so we'll let him help close it. But remember, though, it's still a secret."

"What are you three cooking up?" Matt asked as he and his fiancee approached. "Gramps, I need to get Laura home. She has an early morning show to do tomorrow. She's filling in for the weekend guy while he's vacationing in Hawaii for two weeks.

"Don't be such a stranger, Matt. And bring this pretty young lady around every once in a while. I realize that Harley has had you real busy taking care of the stores while he's been building that new house, but you know full well you're always welcome at the Whitefox home."

Everyone was waving and shouting their goodbyes to Matt and Laura as Fossendocker and Leonard made their way back to the fire pit.

"Lenny, don't you say a word about the growling box to anybody, you got that." Fossendocker was speaking just barely loud enough for his buddy to hear. "We don't want Gramps to have any trouble."

"Hey, Dock," Leonard whispered back, "just what is a growling box, anyway?"

"I'm not exactly sure," he replied, "but it's a big secret. And Gramps is pretty worked up about it, says he's going to give Mr. Raddnick a lickin'."

At that moment Fossendocker caught sight of Ralph and Becky, still down by the creek, still holding hands. "Just look at those two, Lenny." Still whispering he added, "that love-letter's not much good now, is it? I'll have to get rid of it. If Ralph knew I had it, he'd break my neck. Yours, too, Lenny, 'cause you read it, too. Besides, it looks like he really likes her." That same uneasy feeling that he'd experienced a few days before was visiting again. That little something that was discouraging him from giving Ralph a hard time about his sweetheart.

"Can you believe that Laura Livingston?" Ruby was saying to her sister and sister-in-law. "She's sure not the same girl I knew in high school. She grew up to be so pretty and smart."

"Well I think she's right," spoke up Mrs. Bill, "I think you should consider writing a book. You have a wealth of knowledge in that head of yours."

"So do I," stated Opal.

"I think so too, Aunt Ruby." Jewel had just joined the other three ladies. "That was a wonderful story tonight. I can't even imagine going through the things Grandmother Virginia went through when she was a child."

Ruby seemed embarrassed all over again. "Well I was flattered, and I certainly appreciate your confidence. But telling a story to your family members and writing a book for the general public are two completely different things. To be totally honest, though, I've been thinking about a book for a few months. Thomas thinks I should go for it."

The other three ladies clapped their hands together and offered words of encouragement and support.

It was well after dark by the time everything was cleaned up and the chairs stored back under the protective roof of the shelter. Sadness, along with some tears, were not well hidden as brother and sister, nieces and nephews, as well as in-laws said their goodbyes to Ruby, Faith, and Henna. They would be heading home to Oklahoma the next morning. Their stay had been much too short.

CHAPTER 8

At exactly eight o'clock Gramps pulled into the driveway. Fossendocker burst through the front door, cleared all three front steps in a single bound and was in the truck trying to stave off an Indian haircut, even before his mother was out the door. She made her way to the driver's side of the old truck shaking her head at the scuffling pair inside. At least the grandchildren help keep them young, she thought of her own parents.

"I didn't know how long you all would be gone so I packed a few sandwiches and some chips." She reached in through the open window and dropped the brown paper bag into her dad's lap. This brought the horseplay to an end, for the time being. "You're own your own as far as something to drink."

"I've got the drinks covered," replied Gramps. "I'll have him home sometime before bedtime." The old truck engine roared to life as it has done many thousands of times since 1982. "Let's go get L.L."

Mrs. Bill watched the old brown truck, cane poles wagging in the back, as it chugged down the street toward the Duvall's. "I wish he would buy himself a new truck," she said out loud, but she knew that wasn't going to happen.

***

The floor moaned as the three stepped through the doorway of the hardware store. "Dorsey Raddnick, I'm here to give you a lickin'," announced Gramps in a boisterous manner. Both boys quickly looked at Gramps, and then at the gentleman behind the counter. "So come take it like a man." Mr. Raddnick closed the drawer of the cash register with enough force that it could have been heard even in the far corners of the store. He squared his shoulders, and started their way. "But first I want to introduce you to my grandson and his friend."

Gramps gave Mr. Raddnick a hardy handshake, as he does everyone, no dead-fish handshakes for him. Gramps always puts some grip into it. "This is my grandson, Fossendocker, he's Pearl's and Harley's youngest boy. I call him Dock, this young fellow is Leonard Lee Duvall, and I just call him L.L."

Offering his hand, Mr Raddnick said, "you must be Paul Duvall's boy, you look so much like him there's no way he could deny you. Okay if I call you L.L., too?"

Leonard managed a bashful, "Yes sir," as he shook the man's hand.

"And this young man, I've met before. Actually, I had the pleasure of selling him a new grease gun a few days ago. I understand that his last grease gun met with unfortunate circumstances." Fossendocker could feel the flush that came to his cheeks, but still he managed to maintain eye contact with the man who had him by the hand.

"Yes, I know," said Gramps, "and that brings us to this. Dock said you called me an Injun."

"Yeah, I reckon I did," answered Mr. Raddnick. "As a matter-of-fact, I recall accusing you of stirring up trouble, too."

"Well, I'm here to give you a lickin' on account of that. I hope you've got a fresh pot of coffee and some of those good donuts from Apple's Bakery."

"Ernie, how about watching the store for a while, will ya?" A skinny, red-faced lad looked around the end of an aisle upon hearing the request, but he never spoke. "Trying to teach the store business to my grandson; he might stand a chance of learning it if I could keep him of that blasted laptop computer long enough."

Fossendocker and Leonard followed the two older gentlemen to the far corner of the store, where they sat down at a small table with a checker board between them. There they dove into a game of checkers. The two boys could only stare in amazement as Gramps and Mr. Raddnick moved their checkers at breakneck speed. They had never seen anything like this before, it was as if they were not planning any of their moves, but obviously they were, and within a minute the game was over. Gramps had three men left, Mr. Raddnick had none.

"I told you I was going to give you a lickin'." Gramps glanced up at the smiling faces of the two boys and gave them a wink.

Mr. Raddnick hung his head in mock shame. "I guess I deserved that lickin' after calling you an Injun." He then invited the boys to pull up a couple of straight back chairs and enjoy a fresh donut.

"Dorsey and I go way back, like you two boys. We've been best friends ever since the first grade of school. We used to get into so much mischief. Why it's a wonder our folks hadn't disowned us."

"Yep, that's right Joseph, but we sure did have a lot of fun, and we still do from time to time."

"Dorse, do you really think we should tell these fellows about the growling box?" Gramps asked his best friend. "You know if word got out we could be in big trouble."

Mr. Raddnick leaned forward studying the faces of the

135

boys. "I think they look pretty trustworthy, don't you?"

"I suppose so." Gramps finished the last bite of his donut and washed it down with coffee. "We were a little older than you two are right now, maybe thirteen or fourteen. Anyway, we were camping out at Camp Seminole one weekend when we got the bright idea that we would slip over to the dairy farm and play a trick on the two girls that lived there. The Tinsley girls....one was our age and the other a year or two younger."

Mr. Raddnick spoke up, "We knew the girls would be going to the barn to do their chores. You see, I was kind of sweet on the oldest girl and I'd been talking to her at school. So I also knew that they were in the habit of practicing their singing after they finished their chores. They would sing to their daddy's mules. Can you just imagine that, singing to a pair of mules?"

"Really, all this mess was my Daddy's fault," said Gramps, "'cause if he hadn't made that growling box, we wouldn't have been there that night......well, maybe we would have." Both men chuckled. "Anyway, we snuck up behind the barn real quiet like and struck a chord on that growling box. Boys, let me tell ya, with that one little growl the singing *stopped*. One more time on the growling box and the screaming *started*. And then one more good, loud growl, just for good measure, and those two girls almost ran *through* the barn doors. They were screaming at the top of their lungs and running wide open. Those poor girls made it all the way to their house in about five seconds. We were about to bust a gut laughing. Later on we heard that Mr. Tinsley's mules broke down their stall door and followed the girls to the house." Both men chuckled again. "Well, we didn't see that, but we sure heard those mules making a bunch of fuss. Didn't we, Dorse?"

"That prank was the best we ever pulled. It still makes me laugh when I think about it," added Mr. Raddnick. "But the funny part of our evening was over. Next thing we knew those girls' daddy was coming across the yard with a shotgun in his hand. And we could hear their mother on the telephone screaming something about a bear, or some kind of beast. We just barely got back in the woods and got hid real good before Mr. Tinsley came around the barn with his double-barrel shotgun and a flashlight. We finally snuck around onto higher ground so we could watch what was going on. Pretty soon the sheriff showed up along with two truck loads of men. All of them with flashlights and guns."

"I'm telling you," said Gramps, "those girls were scared, but so were we! You might say that our little stunt backfired on us. We hightailed it back to the creek as fast as we could, but when we got back to our camp, my Daddy was sitting there waiting for us. He had gotten word that there was a beast on the loose. Well, he knew just what kind of beast it was *and* where to find it. He didn't say a word, he just looked at us real hard, took my growling box and went home. He hid that thing in the smokehouse and it took me a year or two to find it."

Mr. Raddnick chuckled. "I'm pretty sure most everybody's long forgot about that by now. But I'm very sure there's one person that will never forget."

Gramps laughed out loud and interrupted Mr. Raddnick. "He married her. The crazy man married the oldest Tinsley girl. If she ever found out it was him that scared the life out of her and her little sister that night—"

"Him!" shouted Mr. Raddnick. "You were in on it, too, old buddy."

"That's why we have to keep it a secret," added Gramps.

"I bet that was really funny," said Fossendocker. "Could you make us one of those growling boxes?"

"Wouldn't have to," answered Gramps. "I've still got the original, and it still works just like it did when my Daddy made it, more than fifty years ago. But boys you have to understand, I can't turn you loose with a growling box. A growling box is a serious matter."

"It sure is," added Mr. Raddnick. "That thing could have got our tails shot that night." Mr. Raddnick rubbed his shinny bald head. "I sure would like to give Roberta another dose of that growling box for causing all my hair to fall out, but I'd be afraid she'd have a heart attack."

All four had a good laugh before Mr. Raddnick said, "Ah, the good ole days, Joseph. Too bad we didn't have these two skeesters to run with back then. They seem like a bunch of fun.

"They are," declared Gramps, "they truly are. But right now we have an appointment with some fat blue gill bream over at Pig's Eye. Can you fix us up with some crickets?"

Gramps asked Fossendocker and Leonard to fetch the cricket box from his truck. The cricket box was a cylinder shaped container made from screen wire with a funnel shaped top that screwed off and on. There was a cork attached to a string in the small end of the funnel shaped top. Pull out the cork and there was a hole just large enough to allow one cricket to crawl out.

On the way to the truck Leonard said to his best friend. "Man, you are so lucky. Your Gramps is so much fun. I hope I get to see that growling box some day."

"I hope so, Lenny. I hope we both get to see it," added Fossendocker. "I don't know though, the way Gramps sounded, we may not."

Mr. Raddnick tossed the cricket box to Gramps. "There's a hundred or so in there, maybe that's enough to keep you three busy for a while." He did not want to accept any money from his best friend but Gramps won out by leaving it on the counter, along with the explanation that the cricket supply man had to be paid, too.

A few minutes later Gramps, Fossendocker, and Leonard pulled out onto the highway with Mr. Raddnick standing in the doorway of the old hardware store waving goodbye, and wishing he was going fishing with them.

"We'll stop by the barn and hook up to the boat and then we'll be on the way. Didn't figure there was any reason to drag it all the way over here and back, since we go right by there anyway. Just remember, L.L., keep an eye on that old goat."

"Don't worry, Gramps, I will." Leonard thought back to his last visit to the barn. He had lost his race to the fence with Scooter, and he'd worn a bruise for several days as a reminder.

With the little boat trailer securely hooked to the hitch, Gramps stopped the boys before they could get back into the truck. "Come inside, I want you both to see something."

"What is it, Gramps?" The boys were looking around as the old gentleman sat down on a hay bail.

"Right there." He motioned toward a wooden box sitting on the adjacent hay bail. "That's the growling box."

A simple wooden box, about twelve inches by twelve inches and about eighteen inches tall. Very tightly stretched leather covered one end while the other was open. Through a very small hole in the center of the leather there was a string about forty inches long. Obviously the string was tied to something to prevent it from slipping through the hole in the leather.

"That's it," exclaimed Fossendocker, "that's the growling box. I've seen it lots of times but I didn't know what it was."

"How does it work?" asked Leonard as he examined the box from every angle, finally pulling on the string.

"My daddy told me that some hunters would use the growling boxes in the swamps. They would sit the open end on the surface of the water then pinch the string between their thumb and forefinger, like this, and then slide their fingers up the string. A deep, growling noise rumbled from the box as Gramps demonstrated the technique. You have to put bees wax on the string to make it work, and the sound of the growl can be changed by the amount of pressure you put on the string. Stories have it that some hunters could call up a gator using one of these. Mostly, I think kids just played with them."

Leonard made a nice growl after only his second try, but it took several tries before Fossendocker got the hang of it.

Fifteen minutes later they were backing the boat into Pig's Eye Lake, the boys still laughing about who all they would like to scare with the growling box.

"Mr. Yoder's boat launching ramp is in pretty bad shape." Gramps was having some difficulty keeping the trailer wheels out of a deep rut that had formed in the gravel ramp. "He's gotten too old and in failing health to keep it up. One day soon we'll bring a load of gravel and fix it up for him."

"It's too bad your boat doesn't have wheels on it," sang out Fossendocker, "you could just unhook it and roll it into the water."

"That would be awesome!" yelled Leonard.

"Actually, that sounds like a good idea," Gramps agreed.

Later that day while sitting under a giant weeping willow tree, the threesome were enjoying sandwiches that Fossendocker's and Leonard's moms had fixed. There were at least two dozen nice sized bream in a five gallon bucket. Their first two hours of fishing had been very productive.

"Here Dock," Gramps handed him the sunscreen that his mom had packed in their lunch bag, "better put some of this on. You too L.L., you don't want your arms and faces to get sunburned."

"Hey, Gramps," his grandson was trying to rub in a generous amount of sunscreen on his nose and cheeks, "why is this lake called Pig's Eye Lake?"

Gramps chuckled. "Well, Mr. and Mrs. Yoder moved here some thirty odd years ago. Ruby was about three and she was with me the first time I met them, at the hardware store. Mrs. Yoder just had to stop and tell me what a pretty little girl she was. They had just moved here from Baltimore and had not become accustomed to a more relaxed way of dressing, so Ruby asked her if they were going to church. They looked like they could have been because to us they were dressed up. We've been friends ever since. Anyway, Mr. Yoder sold some property in downtown Baltimore for a ton of money and came out here and bought this chunk of land. He was in his mid-fifties and had done well enough to retire, so he made up his mind to live here and breath fresh air for the rest of his days.

140

And that's exactly what he's doing."

Both boys looked dumbfounded.

"But that didn't answer your question, did it?"

They both shook their heads, no.

So, Gramps continued. "Now keep in mind that all this is according to Mr. Yoder. I never asked his wife." Gramps chuckled. "I'm never gonna ask her. Anyway, after the Yoder's built that fine house we came by on the way in here, he broke the news to her one morning at breakfast that he was going to build this lake. Normally Mrs. Yoder was a pretty easy going lady, but since it was much too early in the morning to be discussing such matters, and being that she was having a bit of a hard time adjusting to her new surroundings, she jumped up from the table and screamed at him, 'In a pig's eye you're going to build a lake!' As you can see, though, he did build this lake. Naturally, he named it Pig's Eye Lake. Mrs. Yoder was so mad at her husband that the day they started building the dam she packed a suitcase and went back to Baltimore to stay with their daughter. It took her three or four months to get over her mad spell and come back. But when she did, she came back with a new outlook on life. Mrs. Yoder came to love this place and the community, and she is very much loved in return. She planted this tree, along with many others on this property, and this became her favorite place to fish. The sweet old lady can out fish her husband, or either one of us, any day of the week."

"That's another good story, Gramps," stated Fossendocker, with Leonard also voicing his approval. Soon they were all back to fishing.

"There's just something special about fishing with a cane pole," said Gramps as he put another cricket on his hook. "A good, slender cane pole is just limber enough to make these one pounders feel like five pounders. Don't you fellows think so?"

"The bucket is more than half full, Gramps," said Leonard, as he dropped in another fat fish. "Just how many are we going to catch today, anyway?"

"That's really up to the fish," replied Gramps. "But we're going to have a big fish fry sometime this summer, so I'd have to say the fish will probably quit biting before we have enough."

And quit they did. Half an hour later it was like a switch had been turned off. The three anglers tried another half hour without a single bite. An hour after that they were back at the barn helping Gramps, mostly by staying out of his way, filet the catch of the day.

"When are you going to have that big fish fry?" Leonard asked Gramps, then before he could answer he added. "I hope you invite me, I really like fish."

"Well, L.L., of course you're invited," exclaimed Gramps. "You are welcome here, anytime." Gramps then explained to the boys that he was planning the fish fry for Labor Day weekend. "My sister, Anna, and some of her family are coming from Texas, and several of my cousins are coming up from Florida. I haven't seen any of my cousins in three or four years. I'm looking forward to seeing them."

"Do you think Aunt Anna and your cousins will tell any family stories while they're here, Gramps?" The boy was already excited about that possibility.

Gramps chuckled. "Son, you'll probably be sick of stories before they head back home."

"No way, Gramps, no way."

Later that night, Fossendocker drifted off to sleep thinking about how much fun the day had been. Lenny and Gramps, he thought, my two best friends in the whole wide world.

CHAPTER 9

June soon faded into July and Independence Day was celebrated all over Collie County with cookouts and parties. The day was capped off with the annual fireworks display at Walkers Park. And as the warm July days were quickly melting away, Fossendocker had somehow managed to stay out of trouble, or at least his mischievousness had not caught up with him.

He and Leonard had kept the streets of Olde Towne hot with their bicycles. Much to the irritation of the residents, they'd left multiple skid marks on most everybody's driveways. They had also spent considerable time spying on Ralph and Becky, who were spending time together during the evening hours strolling around the neighborhood holding hands. Sometimes they would borrow Mr. Roebock's swing that was situated at the edge of his front yard.

Mr. Roebock had hung the swing there many years earlier, from a frame built of substantial timbers, right in the middle of three maple trees that he'd planted. The maple trees are now more than twenty years old and large enough to provide shade for the swing area throughout the day. Several times a day Mr. Roebock sits in his favorite place to watch his Yorkshire Terrier scamper around the yard, and wave at the passers-by. Neighbors claim that it's the same Yorkie that the Roebock's had when they bought that house in 1987. Even Fossendocker knew better than that.

When Ralph and Becky, now known as the *lovebirds*, chose to sit in the swing, Fossendocker and Leonard would, sometimes, hide in the shrubbery. From there they could sneak close enough to hear their conversations. Not that they ever said anything worth listening to. It was almost always stuff like, so and so likes so and so, or so and so is mad at so and so. Useless conversation, as far as these two boys were concerned.

Nonetheless, through their spying, Fossendocker came to the conclusion that, not only did Ralph like this girl, he actually enjoyed spending time with her. He still did not understand how all this boy, girl stuff works, but he did understand the fringe benefits of the courtship. At least from his prospective. Both Ralph and Becky were much more tolerant of him. So, the faithful decision was made to destroy the love-letter he'd found some weeks earlier. Fossendocker fed the letter to his dad's paper shredder, and although Ralph had turned their bedroom upside-down looking for it, the fate of the missing love-letter would forever be a mystery to him.

Besides, Fossendocker had a lot more important things to worry about than Ralph and Becky: Things like moving to the new house, starting a new school, and making plans for the annual camp-out on Labor Day Weekend. At the moment the camp-out topped the list.

Progress on the new house was moving along very smoothly. Everything was on schedule and basically all that remained to be done was some of the landscaping and pouring the concrete driveway. Mrs. Bill had already started packing boxes, trying to get a head start of the late July move. Fossendocker was seriously heartsick about having to leave his old neighborhood and his best friend, but at the same time he felt an excitement.

Emotions that were truly difficult for an eleven-year-old to understand.

On the other hand, the camp-out was something his best friend and he had been looking forward to for weeks. For the last two Septembers, Fossendocker and Leonard had camped out on Brightwell Creek on Labor Day Weekend. Naturally, Mr. Bill had always accompanied them. This marked the end of their summer fun and games and the return to the seriousness of their school work. This year, however, the boys had pressured their parents to let them make the camping trip on their own. Still feeling that they were too young for such an adventure by themselves, they agreed to let them go if Ralph and Thurson would also go. Much to their surprise, and delight, the older boys agreed to go along. Camping out and Gramps' big fish fry on the same weekend....what more could they ask for?

"You know we're moving next week, don't you, Lenny? And school starts back a couple of weeks after that."

"Yeah Dock, I know," was Leonard's solemn reply.

They'd just cruised past Ralph and Becky sitting in Mr. Roebock's swing for the eight time, but even the chance to pester the teenaged couple lacked its usual appeal. It hadn't helped matters, either, seeing their moms sitting at the kitchen table earlier that day with tears flowing down their cheeks. They were talking about how strange it was going be, no longer living close together. In spite of their attempts, things had gotten a little emotional.

"Man, I don't know anybody at Midway," Fossendocker said, "except that weird cousin of yours."

"He's not really weird, Dock, he just has a weird name. You know, kinda like this other guy I know." Fossendocker glared at his friend. "Hutchens Fuller Albright," continued Leonard, "I think he was named after his granddaddy or somebody. Everybody just calls him Hut."

Leonard rolled to a stop and sat down on the grass. "Dock, let's talk about something a little happier, okay. Like maybe the camp-out or something. My dad told me that when he was a kid, and went on camping trips, they would wrap hamburger patties in aluminum foil and cook them in the fire coals. They cooked potatoes and corn on the cob the same way. Even onions, too, he said. I don't know about onions but Dad says they're great; you cut them up in pieces the size of his thumb, wrap them up with a chunk of butter and salt and pepper, and let the hot coals do the work."

"You're making me hungry, Lenny. That sounds real good. I might even try a piece of onion. Maybe we could do that instead of hot dogs this year."

"Well, Dad, says," Leonard added, "the beauty of all this is that you can get everything ready at home and throw it in a cooler. Everything is wrapped up so you don't have to touch any of the food you're cooking with your grubby hands. Plus, you don't have any dishes to wash."

"I like the no dishes part." Both boys were smiling again, in much better spirits than they were a few short minutes ago. "I'll talk to Ralph tonight; I think he'll like the idea, too. Shoot, Lenny, you might even have to try some onion."

The boys chatted away about the camp-out and the fish fry scheduled for that same weekend. Leonard asked his best friend question after question about Gramps' cousins, most of which he couldn't answer. He could only share with his pal what little his grandfather had shared with him. Still, their minds were dwelling on much more pleasant things than they would have to deal with the following week.

Bright and early the next morning Fossendocker was knocking on the Duvall's front door. "Hey Lenny," he shouted, "hey Lenny, get up you lazy bum."

"I'm up," came Leonard's response as he opened the door, "I was having some cereal. What's up, Dock?" Leonard sniggered, ignoring the cross look he was getting, because he knew how much Fossendocker disliked that infamous cartoon question.

"Gramps called last night and told me that one of his cousins is bringing his grandson. His name is Tommy Whitefox and he's about the same age as we are. Gramps wanted to know if we would invite him on our camp-out."

The boys hashed it over for a few minutes and decided to invite Tommy and Leonard's cousin, Hut, as well. Fossendocker figured it would be a good opportunity for him to get to know his future classmate.

The next two days were filled with planning the camp-out, working on the menu, setting up their tent to make sure it was in good repair, and airing out their sleeping bags. This was going to be the best camp-out yet!

***

"Sadie, I really need to get these boxes packed up before tomorrow, you know." Mrs. Bill was stuffing towels and wash cloths into a cardboard box, leaving only enough in the linen cabinet to meet their needs for one more day.

"Ah, come on, Pearl, if you don't show up Miss Millie will wonder why, and in a day or two you'll be sorry you missed it. You know I'm right." Mrs. Duvall put on her best sad face. "Besides you need the break, and I'll help you when we get back."

Mrs. Bill dropped her shoulders in surrender, "Oh, alright, Sadie. Let me freshen up a bit and put on some decent cloths, if I can find any in this mess." Both ladies looked up and down the hallway; it was lined with cardboard boxes. "The whole house looks like this!" exclaimed Mrs. Bill.

"It'll be okay," assured her long time friend. "I'll round up the boys while you get ready."

"Holy smokes, Pearl, where am I going to park? It looks like everyone from three counties is here," declared Mrs. Duvall, "I don't think I've ever seen downtown Plainville so full of cars or people."

"Mama and Daddy are here somewhere," said Mrs. Bill, "they said it would be best to park behind the courthouse. Everyone is supposed to gather at the library parking lot, then walk over and stand in front of Miss Millie's. The mayor has this all planned out. He says that we can gather in the street in front of the cafe and Miss Millie will never notice a thing while she's getting lunch ready."

"Yeah right," said Mrs. Duvall, "you could put a pillowcase over her head and she would still know what's going on."

"Well yeah, that's what I say. But you know the mayor, he has it in his head that she won't know a thing until she comes to the window to turn her closed sign over to the open side."

"I don't know why she has that sign, anyway," added Mrs. Duvall, "the whole world knows when she's open."

Both ladies chuckled, and continued to look for a parking space.

"You two sure are quiet back there." Mrs. Bill glanced over her shoulder at Fossendocker and Leonard safely buckled in the back seat.

"We're looking for Grams and Gramps," stated her son, without even as much as a glance at his mom.

"Look!" shouted Mrs. Duvall, causing her best friend to jump with surprise. "That policeman is backing out of that space, what luck."

They had their parking space but still had seen no sign of Grams and Gramps, when suddenly Fossendocker yelled, "They're over there on the steps to the library." He and Leonard were already heading their way.

The two ladies exchanged puzzled looks. "How did he spot them all the way over there?" asked Mrs. Duvall.

"Beats me, Sadie, sometimes I think he and Daddy have some kind of built-in wireless connection."

What they didn't realize was that Fossendocker had not seen his grandfather, he had *heard* him. Gramps had actually

148

spotted them as they were exiting the car and let out a loud whistle in the form of a four-note bird call. It had taken Fossendocker almost two years to master this bird call, but master it he had, and now he and Gramps had their special whistle. Of course the loud whistle meant nothing to the adults, but when it struck Fossendocker's ears, his eyes immediately began to search the area. A second bird call was all it took for him to zero in on its source.

To an outsider this surely would have been an odd sight. Hundreds of men, women, and children moving as one giant mass of humanity. Down Jefferson Street, across Washington Square, the home of the Collie County Courthouse and the Veterans Memorial, and spilling onto Franklin Avenue. Some carried signs and banners with a variety of messages. Things like, 'Thank you Millie for Fifty Years' and 'Millie McCray for Mayor.'

"I wonder what the mayor thinks of that one," Gramps pointed and chuckled at the idea of Millie McCray running for mayor.

"Look at that sign Ole Sam is carrying." Grams was trying not to laugh out loud, with only limited success. Ole Sam, at sixty-something, or so he claimed, was not seen around town very often except during fresh produce and fruit season. Not much was known about the particular old gentleman with the long white beard, outside of the fact that he always wore long sleeved plaid shirts and bib overalls. Sam Panders just showed up in Collie County in the mid-fifties with his pickup truck and some money. He paid cash for a ten and a half acre track of land a few miles outside of Plainville. He'd built a small wooden house, planted a garden, and an orchard on his property, and pretty much kept to himself. In spite of his shyness, he always had the best looking vegetable garden in the county. Ole Sam, as he prefers to be called, had indeed grown old, as he sold his vegetables, apples, and pears from the tailgate of his antique truck.

Everyone turned to look at Ole Sam's sign, and chuckled as

Fossendocker read it aloud, "'Millie, will you marry me?'"

"The old rascal's been head-over-heels over Millie McCray since the day they met. There's no telling how many times he's proposed to her down through the years, and she's turned him down every time. If she said yes today he would probably have a heart attack and fall dead."

They all chuckled again but quickly turned their attention to a tractor pulling a trailer. On the trailer a makeshift stage had been constructed. The driver situated the trailer so that it sat across both lanes of Franklin Avenue. This is where Mayor Fitzwaller would make his speech. Stretched from one end of the stage to the other was a huge banner proclaiming it to be 'Millie McCray Day.'

"I don't know what Miss Millie is going to think about all this attention," said Mrs. Bill, "she's a pretty private person you know."

Gramps, Grams, and Mrs. Duvall all nodded and voiced their agreement.

"Hey look over there," exclaimed Fossendocker. "There's some more of those guys with the funny looking hats, like the man we saw at Mega Mart. Who are those guys, Gramps?"

"They do a lot of charity work, Dock, especially for the children's hospital and the children's home at Lincoln." Gramps agreed to tell him more about them when they were in a quieter place, which satisfied Fossendocker's curiosity for the time being.

The crowd continued to swell, as the street in front of the little cafe and the courthouse grounds filled with people. "I think my watch is a couple of minutes fast but it says eleven-twenty-two," said Gramps, consulting his wristwatch. "She'll flip that sign over at exactly eleven-thirty."

"Dock, look at that," Leonard said excitedly while tugging at his friends arm. "There's a TV truck parked over there past the trailer. It says channel seven news. And there's a lady talking to the mayor. Let's go check it out." The boys darted off as they heard, "don't go too far," coming from their mother's lips.

"That's Matt Stamp's new wife, isn't it?" asked Gramps.

Fossendocker and Leonard ran up near Laura just as she was finishing her interview with the mayor. She gave them a little wave, below camera view.

"Mayor Stanley Fitzwaller, ladies and gentlemen," she said, looking into the camera. "Thank you very much Mr. Mayor for your time. Now in case you've just joined us, this is Laura Livingston-Stamps live from downtown Plainville with special coverage of Millie McCray Day. I can't believe how many people are here." The cameraman swings around showing the crowd and slowly pans northward up the street as Laura continues to talk. "There are hundreds of people here," she said excitedly, "at least eight or nine hundred on Franklin Avenue already, and there's no telling how many more are in Washington Square. What a testimony to the love and respect this community has, including myself, for Millie McCray."

With the camera now fixed back on Laura, she continued. "We have a couple of minutes so let's speak to these two young gentlemen." She took three steps toward Fossendocker and Leonard, the camera following. "I see you're out to celebrate this special day with your families?" They both nodded. "Tell us your name and where you go to school." Laura leaned over slightly and held her microphone in front of Fossendocker's face.

"My name is Fossendocker Bill. You can call me Dock. I will be in the sixth grade at Midway Middle School."

"Very good, Dock," said Laura, giving him a big smile, "and you are?"

"I'm Lenny. I'll be in the sixth grade at Plainville Middle School."

"So, Dock, I'm aware that you actually attended elementary school here at Plainville, as did you, Lenny, right?" Both boys nodded. "So tell me something fellows, has Miss Millie ever read for your class?"

Both boys nodded again and said that she had read to them,

lots and lots of times.

Laura repositioned herself between the boys in a semi-kneeling fashion so they were somewhat on the same level. "Well guess what guys, I went to elementary school at Midway, and she read for us, too. In fact, it's estimated that she has visited the schools in our area, for the purpose of reading to the students, more than *two thousand* times over the past thirty-five years." Laura gave both boys a little hug and thanked them.

The cameraman panned to the front of the little cafe. "We'll have other facts to share with you as coverage continues. Miss Millie will turn her open sign in just a couple of minutes. Being a TV show host, and sometimes news reporter, I know that I'm not supposed to show emotion and all that, but I can't help being as excited as everyone else."

"*Roger*," Laura yelled at her cameraman, "there she is, at the door, looking out."

Without turning her sign to the open side, Millie slowly opened the front door of the cafe and took one step forward. Gazing out at the sea of smiling faces, she read signs and banners with her name on them. She saw the stage occupied by the mayor and others, dressed nicely as if this were some kind of special occasion. She saw the TV camera and the lady reporter. She saw it all, yet she could not believe what she was seeing. Yes, the mayor and Collie County had somehow managed to surprise Millie McCray. Not only was she surprised, she was completely overwhelmed. Half turning around, she looked behind her with a dozen questions written in her expression.

The pretty young lady standing only feet behind her, smiled brightly, "Millie McCray, this is your day. Go now."

Miss Millie turned back toward the waiting crowd, inhaled a deep breath as she tried to make sense of it all, took two more steps and was outside. Thunderous applauds, whistles, and cheers greeted her and went on for almost a full minute.

As the noise level went down a few decibels, the public

address system on the makeshift stage came to life. "Ladies and gentlemen.......ladies and gentlemen, as Mayor of this fine city of Plainville, it is my extreme pleasure to declare and proclaim that from this day forward the twenty-eight day of July shall forever be known as Millie McCray Day." Another roaring round of applauds and cheers interrupted the mayor. "Miss Millie....," the mayor tried to quiet the crowd, "Miss Millie McCray this is your day. Please come forward and be honored."

With some effort Millie began the fifty feet journey to the stage. The mass of people enveloped her, cutting her off from the cafe. There was no turning back now, she would have to address her fans. After she reached the stage the young woman who had been in the cafe with Millie slipped out, closed the door behind her, and melted into the crowd.

The celebration went on for another couple of hours and culminated with Miss Millie making as many chicken salad and peanut better sandwiches as she could, with what she had. She tossed an apron over the cash register and refused to take payment from anyone. Instead she had a bright red coffee can handy and encouraged her customers to donate to the children's home.

Unfortunately, by the time Fossendocker, Leonard, their mothers, and Gramps and Grams made their way into the little cafe, Miss Millie's food supply was exhausted. No matter, they took the opportunity to thank her, and congratulate her on so many years of loyal service to the community.

"Hey, Miss Millie," sang out Fossendocker, "me and Lenny got on TV."

"Lenny and I," she corrected, "and how did you manage that, young man?"

Fossendocker shrugged his shoulders and took a sip from the glass of cold milk she had given him. "She asked if you had ever read for us at school."

Miss Millie laughed and rubbed his fuzzy head. "You've outgrown me reading to you now, Dock. But I hope I'm around to read to your children."

"Knowing you, you will be," said the smooth deep voice of Thad Callahan, a forty-year veteran of the Plainville Police Department, chief for the past eighteen or so. He sat down on the stool next to Fossendocker.

"I'm clean out of food, Chief, I hope you brought your lunch today."

The Chief nodded that he had. "I just wanted you to know that your being so popular sure caused a lot of problems. Every street, every road, in or out of Plainville was clogged up." The Chief winked at Fossendocker. "We estimated there was between twenty-three and twenty-five hundred people within a block of this place. Do you reckon folks love her?" The Chief's question was directed Fossendocker's way.

"I reckon they do, Chief," Fossendocker answered.

The Chief stretched over the counter to gave Miss Millie a big hug and a kiss on the cheek. He whispered something in her ear that made her blush, then made his way back out the door.

So, Miss Millie McCray had finally answered the question she'd been asked a hundred times over the past few months. She had no intention of closing the cafe. Apparently in her opinion, which was really the only one that mattered, she *had* made it in the cafe business.

CHAPTER 10

"My bike's already over at the new house." Fossendocker sat cross-legged on the front lawn watching the moving men load the Bill family belongings onto a big truck. "Dad hauled it over there last night, Lenny, my scooter and skateboard, too. So," he shrugged his shoulders, "I guess this is it."

"This stinks something awful, Dock." Leonard really didn't know what else to say. His best friend in the whole world was about to move off, and his heart was really heavy right now.

"Yeah, it stinks alright. Man, you wouldn't believe how fast these guys can clean out a house. They're almost finished and Mom told me to get Duke and Duchess ready to go at eleven o'clock." Fossendocker stood and started toward the house. "Come check out my room, Lenny. Mom says that it hasn't been this clean in years."

The boys entered the house and were immediately in the mover's way.

"Guys, please stay out of the way," barked Mrs. Bill. "Fossendocker your dad and Ralph are on the way back to get the last load of tools and stuff out of the basement. Be sure to have the dogs ready to go when the moving truck leaves. I need to go then, too, so I can show them where to put all the furniture. Okay."

Fossendocker nodded and ducked into his empty bedroom. The two boys stood in the middle of the room looking around. No bed, no chest-of-drawers, no dresser, and no clutter. "Wow," said Leonard flatly, "I think your mom's right, it's clean." But suddenly they heard shouting from outside the house that caught their attention.

"Pearl! Pearl!" The boy's ears perked up with curiosity as they heard the sound of Leonard's mother's voice. "Can you come outside for a minute, please."

"I wonder what Mom's doing here?" Leonard asked as he and Fossendocker headed for the living room. The boys quickly stationed themselves at the front windows, in an attempt to hear the conversation that was about to take place between their mothers.

Mrs. Bill met her best friend in the front yard. There was excitement in the air, with smiles and laughter. There was even some jumping up and down like a pair of little girls. But, try as they might, the two eavesdroppers could not hear the conversation over the noise the movers were making as they traipsed back and forth.

"What was that all about Lenny? Your mom was sure excited about something," asked Fossendocker.

"Who knows," was Leonard's simple reply. Then the pair headed for the back yard to ready the two Westies for the trip to their new home.

"No, really, Sadie, the timing couldn't be more perfect. The boys can have a little more time together before school starts back. Plus the fact that Lenny will help keep Fossendocker out of my hair while I work on getting the place straightened out. Besides, you two need *and* deserve a vacation."

Mrs. Duvall had just explained to Mrs. Bill that her husband had called from work to tell her that his supervisor was sending him to the company's home office in Denver for a two-day conference. His boss had told him since it was such short notice he would give him the remainder of the week off. Arrangements had already been made for a company car so they could tour the Rockies for a few days. And his secretary had already made their airline reservations. They would leave out Sunday at six in the evening and return the following Saturday night.

"I just can't believe how generous Mr. Jenkins is being, they're even paying for my plane ticket, Pearl."

"Maybe he feels guilty about ruining your vacation plans last year when he gave Paul that promotion," Mrs. Bill said. "You really can't blame Paul for not wanting to leave while he was learning his new job. But whatever the reason, I'm thrilled for you, and you don't have to worry about Lenny while you're gone."

Mrs. Duvall threw her arms around her best friend and thanked her over and over. "Now, what else can I do to help you get packed?"

"You have already been a tremendous help, but if you insist," Mrs. Bill laughed lightly, "I have a couple of coolers in the kitchen; everything in the refrigerator needs to be packed."

With that the ladies were off to the kitchen, chattering away about the Duvall's upcoming trip to the Rocky Mountains.

A little more than an hour later, Mrs. Bill's SUV was packed to the ceiling with everything from bath towels to dogs and a cat. The movers had closed the doors on their big truck and were pulling out of the driveway.

"Tell Lenny and Lenny's mom goodbye Dock, we need to go." Mrs. Bill was already buckled in behind the steering wheel of her car.

"Bye, Lenny's mom. Bye, Lenny," the heartsick boy slid into the front seat beside his mom.

"See ya later, Dock," was all that Leonard could manage to say.

Fossendocker tried to watch his best friend out the back

window but there was so much stuff in the car he couldn't see out. He couldn't see Leonard waving as they drove out of Olde Towne, then drop his head, fighting back tears of sadness with all his might.

"I'll never see my best friend again." Leonard muttered when his mom put her arm around his shoulders.

"Sure you will," his mother answered cheerfully, "you're going to stay with him all next week. Your dad and I are going to Denver for the week." She turned and started up the street toward their house, leaving her son stunned and speechless.

It took a few seconds for his mom's statement to really sink in, but when it did, he scampered up the street to catch up with her. "What do you mean I'm spending next week with him?"

"Your dad has to go to Denver next week, for business. I'm going with him, and we're going to make it a vacation trip. We leave Sunday evening, after we take you to Dock's house. Rhonda will be staying with Aunt Kathy. I hope you're not too upset. Your dad and I need a little time off, you know."

"Upset? Why would I be upset," he exclaimed. "This is like Christmas or an extra birthday or something! Going to my best friend's house for a week; his new house, with his very own room. And new woods to explore and everything." Leonard was almost beside himself with excitement. "Mom, this is the greatest, thanks a million!"

"You're welcome," she replied, "but the one you really need to thank is Dock's mom. It was her idea. I thought it would be okay to lock you in your room for a week. Just leave you some food and water."

Leonard stopped in his tracks, glaring at his mother.

"Just kidding, Lenny," said his mom, laughing at his shocked expression. "But one thing I'm not kidding about is that you had better be on your very best behavior. Pearl is going to have her hands full next week getting things in order at their new house, you know."

"I will, Mom, I promise." Leonard was back to reality, having survived the surprise of being told he was going to his best friends house, and the shocking threat of the being locked in his room for a week. The spring returned to his step. "I need to call Dock and tell him," he continued, "do they have their new phone number yet?"

"Their phone is supposed to be switched today. It's the same number, Lenny, they're only moving five or six miles away. You act like they're leaving the state."

Running ahead of his mom, Leonard grabbed the phone as soon as he entered the house. There was no answer at the Bill home.

"Lenny, sweetheart," said his mom, having caught up with him, "they haven't had time to get there yet. Try again in a little while. You can't use the kitchen phone, though, it has quit working all together."

"Okay Mom." Leonard could not help but flash back to the day his older sister savagely hammered the counter top with the kitchen phone. It was all he could do to keep from laughing. But he knew that would trigger a bunch of questions.

All afternoon Leonard was in his mom's footprints, offering to help her do this and that. He even volunteered to clean his bedroom and take out the trash. It didn't take Rhonda long to pick up on this, and she intercepted him at the garbage cans in the garage.

"Hey, Lenny, doing a little *sucking up*, I see." Her sarcasm was unbecoming and it jabbed him sharply. "You don't have to, you know. Mom really wants to go on this trip with Dad. Why, you could break every window in the house and you would still get to go stay with that *dork* friend of yours. You might be in a body cast, but you'd still get to go."

"Dock is not a dork!" he defended his friend as he felt his face redden and become hot.

"Of course he's a dork," insisted Rhonda, "and so are you,

159

and you're a weasel."

That did it! That really made Leonard mad, and he was not going to take it. "You'd better remember our treaty," he yelled, shaking his finger at her.

"Oh yeah, that reminds me, I have something to show you." Rhonda pulled a small envelope from her pocket, opened it, and dumped its contents into the garbage can. Tiny flakes of paper drifted down and settled on the trash bag that Leonard had just deposited. "It took me a while to find it, and it took me a while to cut it up into pieces this small, but you can say goodbye to your treaty." Rhonda turned to walk away.

Still holding the garbage can lid, Leonard was stunned. "*I'm telling!*" he bellowed, "you just wait till Dad gets home!"

"You don't get how this works, do you, bozo? You can't tell on me now." Her voice was stern and confident. "It's been weeks. You would be in as much trouble as I would for not telling on me in the beginning." She continued on out of the garage.

"This is war, you know!" yelled Leonard. "This is war!" Then to his surprise his sister's head reappeared in the doorway.

Delivering her very best fake smile she calmly said. "Lenny, my sweet brother, this has been war ever since you ripped the arms and legs off my favorite doll." Then she was gone again.

Leonard Lee stared into the garbage can at the tiny bits of paper. I wonder how she got them cut up so small, he thought, before replacing the lid. Retreating to his bedroom, he sank to the floor and leaned back against his bed and tried to recall pulling the arms and legs off Rhonda's doll. Soon, however, he forgot about all that. His thoughts turned to spending the week at Dock's new house, exploring the woods, the creek, and finalizing the plans for the camp-out.

The next couple of days finally dragged by. The Bill's and Duvall's had agreed to have lunch together at the local steakhouse after church. Just before they would deliver Leonard and his load of stuff to Midway.

160

FOSSENDOCKER BILL   GRAMPS AND THE NEW HOUSE

"I can't wait to see their new house." Mrs. Duvall was squirming with excitement as they turned into the newly paved driveway behind the Bill's SUV. "Look at it, Paul, it's so pretty. I love that front porch." They all bailed out and rushed in behind their friends.

For the next half hour the ladies wandered from room to room, making the tour last three time as long as it had taken the men. Their interest was elsewhere. Mr. Bill invited his friend downstairs to his workshop, where he painstakingly explained every workbench, every storage cabinet, and every drawer to Mr. Duvall. Much to his delight, Mr. Duvall, who is quiet handy with tools himself, was very impressed.

In the meantime Fossendocker and Leonard lugged all his stuff to Fossendocker's new bedroom. "Man, what a huge room," said Leonard, "and all to yourself." Leonard had never had to share his room with a brother, and he was glad. Although he had wished for a brother, many times, in instead of the sister he was stuck with.

"Let's go outside Lenny," suggested Fossendocker. "Let's get our bikes and I'll explain the road to you." They were off like a flash, this time avoiding any further instructions from their preoccupied mothers.

"Here's the deal, Lenny." Fossendocker began Leonard's orientation of the area. "This road is called, Brightwell Crossing Road. Dad says it's a loop because both ends are connected to the big road. It goes by our house, crosses the creek, goes by Gramps and Grams, and that's all. Dad says that from one end to the other is a little over a mile. And guess what, Lenny. Nobody can build any more houses because it's all family land, except for a little bit at both ends. Dad says that it's right-o-way, or something like that. There's not many cars on this road, but we still have to be careful."

The boys slowly peddled past the narrow, now gated, road leading to Camp Seminole and on to the bridge spanning Brightwell Creek. Stopping on the bridge, the two boys passed the time watching leafs and sticks float downstream.

"I wonder how long it would take for something to float from Camp Seminole to here?" said Leonard.

"Don't know," answered his buddy, "but we can give it a try tomorrow. We can use one of Ralph's tennis balls."

Both boys sniggered knowing that would hack Ralph off. They crawled back on their bikes and started back toward the new house. Suddenly the sound of a motor filled their ears as a dirt bike raced around the curve in front of them. They both knew it was the same person who had disrupted the cookout a few weeks earlier. The helmet-less, long-haired teen sped past them without even giving them the slightest glance. Fossendocker shrugged his shoulders, indicating to his best friend that he didn't have a clue about this guy.

Once they were back at the new house, Leonard's parents gave him one final set of instructions, which were the same as the first and second sets. Leonard nodded as he was told to use proper table manners, go to bed when he was told, respect and obey Mr. and Mrs. Bill, and so forth.

Mr. and Mrs. Bill assured their friends that their son would be just fine. With that certainty, they said their goodbyes, and were on their way to the airport.

Early the next morning a loud boom of thunder woke Fossendocker with a start. He shook Leonard, "wake up, Lenny, I think it's raining outside."

"Rain! No, that stinks, Dock," said Leonard. They dressed themselves, all the while complaining about the weather, then made their way to the kitchen. To their surprise they were greeted by Mrs. Bill, with a smile, and two glasses of orange juice.

"How did you know we were up?" asked her still drowsy son.

"I went to look in on your sister after that loud clap of thunder, and I heard you two complaining about the weather as I passed your doorway. Don't be overly concerned about this little

162

thunderstorm. It really hasn't rained very much, and the weather forecaster says that it will be gone in a couple of hours. Clear skies will follow; warm and dry for the next few days. Your mom called earlier, Lenny, to let us know they got to Denver safely."

That good news about the weather sat very well with the two boys, and their smiles showed it. Leonard was also relieved to hear that his parents were okay. But being a boy, he didn't let it show very much.

"How about a stack of pancakes? Oh, by the way, Gramps is coming over when the rain stops. He said he wants to show you two some things about these woods."

"All right!" they both said in unison, and delivered to each other a sharp high five. Maybe Ralph and Thurson no longer thought high fives were cool, but they did.

BILL DALE GRIZZLE

CHAPTER 11

Three hours later Gramps was knocking at the door. After handshakes, hugs, a cup of coffee, and a slice of apple pie that his daughter had just taken out of the oven, Gramps was ready to get down to business.

"Boys, what you have to remember about this section of woods is," he pointed to his right, "if you go far enough that way you hit the highway. If you go far enough that way," he then pointed to the left, "you hit the creek. But if you go far enough that way," Gramps pointed straight at the woods behind the new house, "there's no telling what you might find." He looked at one boy, then to the other, their eyes were wide with excitement. "We had better take a little water with us, it's pretty hot and humid today."

Fossendocker and Leonard darted off to fetch a few bottles of water and their backpacks.

A few hundred feet into the forest, which was a mixture of evergreen and hardwood trees, they came across a well-used trail. "This is a game trail, guys. This trail has been used by deer, turkeys, foxes, bobcats, and other kinds of animals for many generations. Animals are mostly creatures of habit, once they make a trail they will very often use it for a long, long time, provided they aren't disturbed and they feel safe. I've been watching critters use this trail since I was your age. Matter of fact, back when I was a boy there weren't many deer and turkeys, almost all of them had been killed off for food. But I had the pleasure of seeing them all along this trail. I couldn't tell anybody outside of the family, though, there were still some folks around that would have slipped in to hunt."

Gramps stopped long enough to inspect a sandy section of soil and directed their attention to a couple of sets of fresh deer tracks. "A doe and her fawn," he said, "look how small the fawn tracks are. Now if you follow the trail that way it will take you between the first and second of the Six Cedar Hills, all the way to the creek. If you follow it that way, it will lead you to an old homestead. There are still a bunch of fruit trees there and a big patch of wild plums. Animals like to hang around old homesteads; copperheads and rattlers like 'em, too. So you best be careful if you find yourself there."

"Gramps," spoke up Leonard, "why do deer like to walk on trails?" The boy looked puzzled, and to the not so woods-wise youngster, this was a legitimate question.

"I know that one," Fossendocker quickly said. "They don't like to go through a briar patch any more than we do. Right Gramps?"

"Yep, Dock, that's part of it. When it's safe, deer often prefer to travel where the walking is easier. They also use their trails to keep up with who's in the neighborhood. You know, they leave their smells behind. But one thing for sure, there's always some kind of cover handy for them to duck into should they feel threatened. That was a good question, L.L., that's how you learn things. So, when you're around me, don't ever be bashful about asking questions. Either one of you."

The threesome continued on slowly with Gramps stopping

every now and then to show the boys something or to explain a tree or a plant. Then they came across an old woods road.

"Where in the world does this old road go, Gramps?" Fossendocker asked. "It looks like someone has been on it. See how the grass is mashed down."

"This old road has been here for more than a hundred years. Shoot, who knows, maybe even two hundred years. The records at the Collie County Courthouse show that this road used to run from Highway 57 all the way to Greenvine. It meandered right along the Sagawata's, and that's why it was called the Mountain View Road. Boys, as far as I know, this is all that's left of that old road. That's why I run over it a couple of times a year with my bush mower. I'm just not ready to let Mother Nature have it back yet, too much history here."

Fossendocker and Leonard hung on every word out of Gramps' mouth. He was a well of knowledge and information, and he enjoyed being with the boys as much as they enjoyed being with him.

"But where does it come out if you go that way?" Leonard asked a split second before his buddy could, and pointed in the direction the threesome were traveling. "If we go back that way," the boy glanced over his shoulder, "wouldn't we be going toward Dock's new house, or maybe the big road?"

"That's exactly right, L.L., actually, that end of the old road is right at the corner of Dock's new yard. I'm surprised that you haven't noticed it, Dock. I guess you've been too busy helping your daddy. But then again, it is kind of hidden by that clump of cedar trees. The other end," Gramps paused for a few seconds looking ahead to the point where the woods swallowed the old road, "maybe we should just go see for ourselves."

With that they struck out northward on Mountain View Road. A few minutes later they stood at the top of Pyrite Ridge looking out across a small meadow of grasses and wild flowers. A half dozen species of birds fluttered around feasting on the seeds

BILL DALE GRIZZLE

and insect that this food-rich meadow offered, while butterflies and honey bees went from flower to flower gathering nectar. Then without warning a doe and her twin fawns burst from their bedding place and bounded into the woods. They had been perfectly camouflaged, hidden amongst the grass and wild flowers, but the three humans had gotten a little too close for comfort.

The threesome stood there for several minutes without saying a word. It was peaceful here.

"Do either of you know what pyrite is?" Gramps finally asked as he sat down on a large flat rock and twisted the top off a bottle of water. He stretched his legs out and massaged his thighs. His legs are not as young as they used to be and walks in the woods made him fully aware of that fact.

"Yeah, Gramps, I know," Leonard quickly spoke up. "It's stuff that's found in the ground that looks kind of like gold. I remember that from science class."

Fossendocker nodded his approval of his friend's answer. "It's called fool's gold, right Gramps?"

"You're both absolutely right. This ridge is called Pyrite Ridge because there's so much pyrite here. Word has it that in the late 1860's or early 1870's some jack-leg found this deposit of pyrite and thought he'd struck it rich. He sacked up a bunch of it, took it to town and tried to pass it off as the real thing. Well the townsfolk ran him out of town, why, they even threatened to tar and feather the poor fellow. But it turned out that he wasn't the dishonest crook folks first thought. He'd fought in the Civil War and was what they called then, shell shocked. Nowadays we know that as a traumatic brain injury. He was probably real close to a cannon ball or something that exploded. Apparently it effected his brain, and his way of thinking. So you see he really didn't mean to do anything wrong, and he wasn't trying to cheat anyone on purpose. Sometimes you just don't know about folks, right boys? But anyway, thanks to him this ridge has a fine name."

"That's a good story, Gramps, but why are there no trees

168

right here?" Fossendocker had already surveyed the meadow and noticed the absence of trees.

"Well, Dock, this is the best I can figure about that. There's a huge deposit of rock here, some of it is just below the surface. Grass and weeds and small bushes can survive in this shallow dirt, but apparently trees can't. You remember the big rocks that seem to be growing out of the ground down by the creek at Devil's Elbow?" Gramps watched as his grandson nodded that he did. "That is where this ridge ends. This whole area has a big vein of rock going through it, and right here on this ridge it's real close to the surface."

"Oh yeah, boys. I almost forgot about something," added Gramps. "Remind me one day soon and I'll take you to visit the talking rock."

"*Talking rock*? Fossendocker laughingly exclaimed. "Rocks can't talk, Gramps."

Gramps chuckled, the way he always chuckled when he had something up his sleeve. Of course this brought on an onslaught of questions from his grandson and the boy Gramps always treats like a grandson.

"I'm not going to tell you anything else about the talking rock. I'm not going to spoil the fun of it. That will be another adventure for another day, okay."

The boys agreed to visiting the talking rock later in the week and for the next few minutes the threesome studied and discussed the different kinds of birds and various plants growing in the meadow. Gramps told them of the time that a couple of older boys had tricked Dorsey Raddnick and him into chewing a mouthful of rabbit tobacco.

"Rabbit tobacco," he said, "which is not even close to real tobacco, grows wild around here in meadows and fields. Those two boys had their chew in a little brown paper bag but they refused to share it with us. They said we had to get our own, so we did. We thought we were going to be big shots by chewing rabbit tobacco like the older guys. Well, I'll tell ya boys, the stuff pretty much taste like dirt, maybe even worse than dirt. While we were spitting and sputtering trying to get that nasty stuff out of our mouths, they were laughing their heads off at us. It turned out the stuff they were chewing was chopped up cabbage they had brought from home. We chased them all the way to the dairy farm but never did catch them."

The boys were laughing at Gramps' story as he stripped a handful of dry, silver-grayish leaves from a slender stalk. "Here, try a bite of this for yourself."

"No way!" They both howled and ran up the road leaving Gramps behind laughing at them.

Just as the two boys reached the far side of the clearing, Fossendocker grabbed Leonard by the shirt sleeve and jerked him to a sudden stop.

"What was that?" He had heard something while running, something in the distance, but he wasn't sure what it was.

"What was what?" asked Leonard.

"Sounded like somebody yelling. You really didn't hear it?"

Leonard shook his head. "I didn't hear anything." But he was now on full alert.

But then they both heard it. The sound was a ways off, they could tell, but still loud and clear enough that they immediately recognized it. Kids.

"Sounds like a bike race, Dock," said Leonard, still a little shocked at hearing the sounds of kids out here in the middle of the woods.

They both turned to look back at a smiling Gramps who had caught up to within twenty feet of the boys.

"Gramps, are there houses out here in the woods? We hear kids playing. Lenny says it sounds like they're bike racing."

"Well, fellows, let's go see." Gramps said boldly as he tromped on by the bewildered youngsters. "There's no telling what we might find on the other side of this stand of oaks."

Fossendocker and Leonard almost had to run to keep up with Gramps as he briskly strode through the oak woods. Keeping up with him made it very difficult to do a lot of looking around, and there was a lot to look at here. The trees standing in this grove ranged in size from as big around as a basketball to enormous. Squirrels scampered around searching the dried leaves for acorns or whatever else they could find to make a meal of. There seemed to be hundreds of birds of all sizes and colors. A crow noisily announced their intrusion, but then the shrill cry of a hawk silenced the pesky crow. The boys very much wanted to stop and explore this fascinating place. But all of a sudden they were out of the trees. They found themselves looking down a gentle, grassy slope, where they saw houses. A subdivision, a street, and this particular street was a cul-de-sac. As the two boys and Gramps gazed down at the neighborhood, young Fossendocker realized that this was not like any cul-de-sac that he had ever seen before. The usual circle of asphalt was very large and in the center was an island of plants and flowers and a trio of crape myrtles, still filled with blossoms. Only three homes shared this cul-de-sac, and even he couldn't help but notice how large the houses and yards were, and how much space there was between each house. He'd never given much thought to financial standing or material things, but it was obvious this place was worlds away from Olde Towne. But still, there were kids here. Three young fellows that appeared to be about the same age as Fossendocker and Leonard were indeed racing their bikes around the island of plants and back up the street.

Leonard Lee quickly recovered from the surprise of seeing homes and other kids here in the middle of nowhere. Or at least it seemed like the middle of nowhere. "Dock," he yelled with excitement, "that's my cousins house. That's where Hut lives."

"No way," his buddy replied. "Gramps, you knew these houses were here, didn't you? That's why you brought us here, isn't it?"

"This is the Bradley Dairy property, or used to be anyway. I tried to buy this property after they shut down the dairy, but the developers and builders had a lot more money than I did. But things have a way of working out. Now that you're living here, Dock, I'm glad these houses are here. There are several boys and girls your age living in this subdivision, and a fellow needs to have some folks around that are close to their age. Am I right?"

"Sure Gramps," answered Fossendocker, but then with concern in his voice he added, "but it sure is a long way over here."

"Actually, boys, it's not that far at all. We did a lot of zigzagging on the way over here so it just seemed like a long way. If you get on the Mountain View Road there at your new house it's only a little over half a mile. On your bicycles, I bet you could be here in about ten minutes."

"Hey, there's my cousin now, he just got on his bike. Hey Hut!" yelled Leonard as loudly as he could. His cousin stopped his bike and turned to look up the hill, wondering who had called his name.

"Let's go visit with him," suggested Gramps as he started down the grassy slope. "Hut and I go way back, you know."

Of course they didn't know that, how could they possibly have known that. And further more, they couldn't even imagine *how* Gramps and Hut would know each other. Shrugging their shoulders at each other, Leonard finally asked, "How do you know my cousin, Gramps?"

"Ah, we met on the Mountain View Road last year. I told him that he and his buddies were welcome to romp around and play in the woods as long as they were careful, didn't leave trash, or burn the place down. Hut has ridden his bike over to my house a couple of times, but he says his friends are a little scared to come along. He also says that they are nervous about going into the woods. I think it's those signs that the government requires us to put up along the property lines."

In the late sixties the Federal Government had declared the

172

Whitefox property to be an official Indian Reservation, this also included a sizable portion of the National Forest. Thus the ominous looking signs that were posted on the property lines demanding that all keep out. "You should get your Aunt Anne to tell you all about that when she's here for Labor Day. It was all her doing, she's responsible for this being a reservation." Gramps smiled at the boys, "You'll get a real kick out of her story."

The two boys and Gramps made their way to where Hut had parked his bike at the edge of his backyard.

"Hey, Chief Whitefox," Hut grabbed his extended hand. "Hey Lenny, what are you doing here?"

Fossendocker could remember a couple of times when his grandfather had been actually been addressed as Chief Whitefox. He thought it sounded pretty cool and he liked it.

"Hut," Gramps started, "this is my grandson, Fossendocker Bill. And L.L. here is spending the week with him while his parents are out of town."

"Yeah, I remember you." Hut addressed Fossendocker with a big smile. "They call you, Dock, right? I saw you at Lenny's house, last summer."

At that point Leonard Lee took charge of the conversation explaining to his cousin how the Bill's had just moved into their new house, and how Dock would be in the sixth grade, the same as Hut, at Midway Middle School.

Hut responded, filling Fossendocker in on the sixth grade teaching staff, who to look out for and who was okay. But the discussion soon shifted to more important things, like the other kids in the neighborhood, their favorite things to do, and such. At that moment Hut's three friends, who were involved in a race, came rolling to a stop some twenty-five feet away.

"They won't come any closer. Dub Dillard Junior has been running his mouth a lot and the guys are a little scared of the Chief. By the way, that's Bunt Barker, Eddie Artwilter, and the guy with the goofy hat is Johnny Ray Shelton."

Fossendocker and Leonard gave them a friendly wave. The three bikers just barely acknowledged their greeting, but did maintain their curious stares. Johnny Ray's hat was pretty goofy, alright. It was one of those straw hats similar to those worn by a couple of the country music singers. The hat was all crumpled up and looked like it had been run over by a truck. But there again, with a name like Johnny Ray Shelton.

"Don't worry about them," said Hut in an attempt to soothe the uneasiness that his cousin and new friend were experiencing. As the three boys rode off once more, he added with confidence, "they'll come around."

The lighthearted conversation went on for another ten minutes before Gramps announced that they had better head back. But before they parted company Fossendocker, Leonard, and Hut agreed to get together the next morning. They had extended to Hut the invitation to camp with them on Labor Day Weekend, and there were lots of plans to be made.

Listening to Fossendocker's and Leonard's constant chatter, Gramps led the way through the oak grove, across Pyrite Ridge, and on through more woods. Before the boys realized how far they had walked they were standing in the back yard of the Bill's new house. Gramps bid farewell to the boys, and told them he was going to go inside to visit with his daughter and Raelynn for awhile before he went home. Halfway in the back door he called back to the boys telling them that he would come back in a couple of days to take them to visit the talking rock.

The two boys were on their bikes within half a minute. But before they had ridden the length of the driveway, Fossendocker stopped.

"Hey, Lenny," he questioned, "I wonder what Hut meant when he said that Dub somebody Junior had been running his mouth? And why would his buddies be scared of Gramps?"

Leonard shrugged his shoulders. "I don't have a clue, Dock. Maybe we should ask him tomorrow."

174

"That's a good idea, Lenny, but you know that I'll probably forget."

Both boys laughed, both knowing that it could be true, and sped down Brightwell Crossing Road in the direction of the creek.

"Dang, Dock," exclaimed Leonard Lee, "we forgot to nab one of Ralph's tennis balls for our experiment."

"Oh no, we didn't," corrected Fossendocker and began digging through his back pack. "We've got two of them." He produced the pair of tennis balls, raising them above his head in celebration of a successful heist from his brother. Sneaking into a big brothers room was risky business. "I snuck into his room while you were brushing your teeth, I even used his magic marker to put our names on them."

Fossendocker and Leonard laughed as they pushed their bikes around the gate blocking the old road that leads to Camp Seminole.

"I don't know why he has tennis balls anyway, Lenny. He doesn't play tennis. I think the only reason he has them is to throw them at me. Better than a baseball or a rock, I guess."

Leonard nodded. "Yeah, I'm glad you didn't wake him up."

"No problem, he went to work with Dad this morning. I'm glad of that though, we don't have to put up with his junk. He's been in a bad mood 'cause he hasn't been able to see his girlfriend."

Fossendocker and Leonard both made faces at the mention of Ralph's girlfriend, and then the mischievous youngsters howled with laughter and made jokes at the expense of their older siblings. Neither one of them could understand the desire to have a girlfriend, or in the case of Leonard's sister, a boyfriend.

"That guy that Rhonda likes is a real creep, Dock. I mean he wears black clothes all the time, and his hair hangs in his face and needs to be washed. He says he's a punk rocker 'cause he plays his guitar so loud. My Dad says he's just a punk."

"Yeah, but you know," said Fossendocker, "Ralph was a lot

nicer to us when he was hanging around Becky, and Becky was a lot nicer, too."

"Well Rhonda's sure not nicer, she's a lot meaner," added Leonard. "I forgot to tell you that she snuck in my room and found our treaty, you know the one you helped me with. She cut it up into tiny little pieces and put it in the trash can." Leonard shook his fist at the open air, "Man, I was so mad....it's not funny, Dock. Stop laughing at me, Dock!"

Feeling the pressure of his best friends glare, Fossendocker managed to bring himself under control before Leonard yelled at him again. With a semi-straight face, he apologized. "I'm sorry Lenny, I couldn't help it. You looked so funny telling me about the tiny little pieces; doing your fingers like scissors, and shaking your fist in the air." He duplicated Leonard's hand gestures.

"There's no way I looked that stupid," snapped Leonard. He straddled his bike and left Fossendocker standing just inside the gate. He couldn't help but laugh again at his sometimes overly-sensitive pal.

Leonard was sitting on a rock overlooking the creek when Fossendocker bicycled up.

"This place is great isn't it Lenny?"

Leonard did not respond. He was not quiet over being laughed at yet.

"And just think about it, Lenny," continued Fossendocker, "someday I could be chief of all this." He spread his arms out in a fashion as to indicate a large area.

Leonard cut his eyes toward his buddy, "Yeah right, you goofball, Chief Fossendocker. Now that *is* funny."

"I'm serious, Lenny!" exclaimed Fossendocker, sensing that the tide had turned on him. Now he may be the one being laughed at.

"Yeah, *chief*. I'm getting hungry," said Leonard, chuckling at his own joke. He retrieved a pack of cheese crackers from his backpack. "You want a pack of crackers, *chief*?"

"You don't believe me, do you Lenny?"

Leonard studied the face of the boy who had been his best friend for eleven long years, and again offered him a cheese cracker. Fossendocker had played a lot of jokes on him and he was all the time trying to feed him some kind of nonsense. As far as he knew, though, Fossendocker Bill was an honest person and would not deliberately tell him a fib. So yeah, somehow this was probably true.

"No!" Leonard half shouted.

Still looking directly at his friend, Leonard could see Fossendocker's face redden with humiliation. Ah, payback is a wonderful thing.

"I'm being serious, Lenny." Fossendocker babbled."It was something that Gramps' sister did when she was in college. She got the government to say that this land is a Native American Reserve, or something like that. You know it's what Gramps was telling us about when we were over at Hut's house, remember....the signs." Fossendocker was pleading his case in earnest, to a seemingly disinterested audience. "Gramps' daddy was the chief and now Gramps is."

"Whatever," Leonard stated rather flatly. Actually this did sounded pretty interesting but he certainly wasn't going to give Fossendocker the satisfaction of letting him know that. "Now can we get going with our tennis ball experiment? What do you say we throw them in at the same time and hurry back to the bridge to see how long it takes for them to get there. We can see whose ball gets there first. Like a race."

Feeling discouraged, unbelieved, and pretty much dejected, Fossendocker pouted. Not until he stole a glance at Leonard, and caught his pal silently laughing at him, did he realize that the joke was on him. He finally laughed, too, and nodded agreement to Leonard's plan.

On the count of three they both tossed their tennis balls into the chilly waters of Brightwell Creek, boarded their bikes and rushed back to the bridge. To their amazement they had to wait less than two minutes until they spotted the fluorescent green tennis balls bobbing into view. One was several seconds ahead of the other as they passed under the bridge, but to their disappointment it was obvious that the marker Fossendocker had used to put their names on the balls was not waterproof. All that was left of their names were faded charcoal-gray smudges that were completely illegible.

Impressed by how quickly the balls had made the trip downstream, the boys discussed how they had floated through the opening between two giant rock formations, known as Pinch Point Pass and around the horseshoe bend before cruising under the bridge. Their friendship had survived their little spat, and once again all was well.

"Gramps says that they should have named Pinch Point Pass something different. He says that it should be named Skint Knuckles Pass, because when you're going through there in a boat or a canoe, if you don't watch what you're doing, you'll get your knuckles skint."

"Boy Dock," laughed Leonard, "Gramps can come up with some good ones, can't he?"

Fossendocker joined his friend in laughter. "He sure can, Lenny. I think that must have really happened to him, though."

Once again the boys hopped on their bicycles and began peddling up the incline toward the new house. Within a couple of minutes they met Gramps as he was heading home. Rolling to a stop he hung his head out the window.

"I had a nice visit with your mother and Raelynn." He called out above the engine noise of his old truck. "She told me to send you two home if I saw you. Your dad is going to have to work late tonight so I think you all are going to meet him in town for pizza." Both boys broke out into smiles. "Now you fellows be real careful out here on this road," Gramps continued, "there's a lot of other crazy drivers out here besides me." With that Gramps

178

sputtered on across the bridge, waving goodbye as he went. The boys watched till he was out of sight then continued on their way.

BILL DALE GRIZZLE

CHAPTER 12

Sitting in the shade on the front porch steps of the Albright house, Fossendocker, Leonard, and Hut were enjoying ice cold lemonade after some hard riding around Bradley Farms.

Bradley Farms, certainly not the most glamorous name for a subdivision, mused Fossendocker. Especially a subdivision like this. He still hadn't gotten over how big the houses were here. And not one thing here reminded him of a farm of any sort. At least the street names in Olde Towne kind of sounded like they fit: Names like Lamplighter Lane or Cobblestone Way. Why, even the flower gardens in this place were tended by professional landscapers, and he had about come to the conclusion that nobody here owned a lawnmower. However, the developers had honored the family who had operated a dairy on this land for five generations, by keeping its name. Fossendocker didn't exactly understand why, but he felt like that was a good thing.

"Ahhhh," said Leonard finishing the last gulp of his drink, "your mom makes great lemonade, Hut. Do you think I could get some more?"

"Sure, Lenny, go on in, Mom's in the kitchen."

Fossendocker had been watching a big, fluffy, white cloud drift across the mid-day sky, while entertaining his thoughts about this place, when he remembered he was going to ask Hut something.

"Hey, Hut," he began, "you remember yesterday when you said that somebody was running his mouth and the other guys were kind of scared of my Gramps? What's that all about?"

Hut took a long deep breath, shaking his head as he slowly exhaled. "That would be, Dub Dillard Junior, the biggest pain in the rear in the whole school, maybe even the whole world. He lives on the highway, sort of off in the trees, in an old double-wide, with his dad, Dub Dillard Senior. He doesn't have a mom, she moved to North Carolina, or somewhere, with his little sister. My Mom says Dub's daddy is a sot, but I really don't know what that is."

Hut paused while taking a couple more swallows of lemonade and studied the face of his new friend.

"No kidding, Dock, he's really a big bully. He and his two friends give everybody a hard time. You'll have to look out for him." Fossendocker cocked his head to the side, questions in his expression. "Seriously, stay out of his way because he'll pick on you, for sure. You know, you being the new guy, and all."

Fossendocker was processing this new information when Leonard exited the house with a fresh glass of lemonade and a handful of cookies to share with the other two.

"Don't worry about it," he said, reading the frowns on their faces, "your mom made me wash my hands."

"Oh yeah, Dock," said Hut through a mouthful of oatmeal raisin cookie, "one more thing about Dub. He's like three or four years older than us. He was in the fifth grade twice, and this will be his third time in the sixth."

Fossendocker could not believe his ears. In his entire school career he had known only one person who had not been promoted to the next grade at the end of the school year. That unfortunate young fellow had managed to fall out of his second story bedroom window while flying paper airplanes, and was in a coma for four and a half months. And now he's being told that one of his class mates had flunked three times before the seventh grade. That's got to be a world record or something, he thought.

Even the poor kid that fell out his window caught up with his original class within a single school year. From the information Fossendocker had so far, he doubted the same would ever be said for Dub Dillard Junior.

Crossing over Pyrite Ridge on the way back to the new house, Leonard dismounted, dropped his bike to the ground, and sat down on the same big flat rock that Gramps had sat on the day before.

"What's up, Lenny?" asked Fossendocker as he studied the odd expression on his friend's face.

"Man, Dock," Leonard was shaking his head, "I think you might be in for it with that guy, Dub. I mean with you being the new guy, with glasses, and with a name like Fossendocker." Leonard shook his head again, "Man, you've had it."

Fossendocker glared at his best friend. "Well I can't help being the new guy. And I sure can't change my name. Gramps gave that to me when I was born, because Mom and Dad couldn't decide on a name. Lucky me, huh."

"Yeah, Dock, I know all that," Leonard paused for a second. "I mean they just don't know what a real good guy you are."

Fossendocker sat down on the rock at a right angle to Leonard and hung his head. "Well, there's not much I can do about it. I'm stuck here and I'm stuck with this new school."

"Well, there is something I can do," exclaimed Leonard as he sprang to his feet. "You wait here. I need to go talk to Hut for a minute." A few second later he was out of sight, peddling his bike as fast as he could in the direction of his cousin's house.

This was actually the first solitary time Fossendocker had

had in days, and he was spending it worrying about what to do about Dub Dillard Junior. He took a deep breath and sighed as he exhaled. When all of a sudden a conversation he'd had with Gramps a few weeks earlier popped into his head. He recalled how he was sitting on the big limb of his Grandfather's favorite old tree, expressing his concerns about going to a new school. He could almost hear Gramps telling him that because of the kind of person he is, everything would be okay, and how he would always have him to turn to, should he need him.

"That's exactly what I'll do," said the distressed boy aloud, "I'll talk to Gramps, he'll help me figure out all this mess." With that little bit of comfort, the worry in his mind, and the heaviness in his heart, flew from him like a dove flushed from the grassy meadow.

The next two days, as full as they were with bike rides and races, exploring the woods and the creek, and solidifying new friendships, flew by very quickly.

***

"Wow, Dock," said Leonard, as they were having a bowl of cereal for breakfast, "our week is almost over."

Fossendocker said nothing. His mind was busy thinking how odd it was going to be starting a new school year without the friend he'd started all five of the previous school years with. He finally nodded his response to let Leonard know that he had been heard, but he chose not to share his gloomy thoughts. It was obvious to him that Leonard was having his own difficulties.

Before they finished their cereal the telephone rang. "Good morning, Mama," Mrs. Bill said, trying as hard as she could to hide the fatigue in her voice. "How are you?" She strolled into the living room with the cordless phone and spoke to her mother for a few minutes, before returning to the kitchen.

"Boys," she said, "Grams said that Gramps is coming over

as soon as gets finished feeding his goat. She says he's coming over here to teach you two some more nonsense. She's invited Raelynn and me over to spend some time with her. We are going to make a batch of fried apple pies later on. After lunch, I would say. I could use a little break from all this, anyway."

"Do you think you could get her to make us a couple of chocolate pies while she's at it?" If Grams could have seen her grandson's pleading eyes there would have been no way she could have resisted.

"I'll see what I can do," replied his mom, giving him a gentle pinch on his left ear.

None of Fossendocker's friends had ever heard of fried chocolate pies, but the mixture of coco, sugar and he didn't know what else, was an old family recipe. Grams folded her ingredients into a very thin and flaky pastry, then fried them to a golden brown in an old iron skillet. They were always a favorite of the young ones, and some of the older ones, too.

***

"Now, I'm going to show you two the easiest way to get to the talking rock. It's not the shortest way, but it's the easiest way. You got me a bottle of water in that pack, Dock?" asked Gramps.

The boy nodded and held up two fingers.

"Good boy, now let's be on our way."

The threesome started up the Mountain View Road and did not stop until they reached Pyrite Ridge.

"Here's where we turn off, fellows." said Gramps, "we go that way, toward the west." Remember this spot in case you ever want to pay a visit to the talking rock again. Glancing at his wristwatch, he nodded and quietly mumbled something to himself.

The boys looked at each other, both wondering what he'd said, but they choose not to ask. Had they asked, Gramps would have explained to them that he was considering the time because the talking rock doesn't like to be disturbed too early in the morning. They quickly caught up with Gramps who was already taking long steps down the ridge on a well-used trail.

"Keep your eyes peeled for a nice straight oak stick. We're going to need one when we get there."

Again the two friends looked at each other. Fossendocker shrugged his shoulders and whispered, "I don't know."

"*There*," Gramps almost shouted. "That's a perfect stick. And right here by the trail, what luck." He grabbed the four feet long stick, barely breaking stride. "We're almost there, boys."

And indeed they were, for within a couple of minutes the boys found themselves looking up at a massive rock protruding from the earth. The huge rock had a shape similar to that of an anvil. Neither boy had ever seen anything like it.

"It's as big as our house," Fossendocker finally managed to say.

"Yep, bigger than a lot of houses," said Gramps. "Eighty-three feet of it sticks out of the ground, it's forty-six feet wide, and it's seventeen feet to the ground from up there." Gramps pointed to the highest point of the rock. "If you fall from there, most likely you're going to need a doctor."

Fossendocker and Leonard were very impressed with the sight of the rock. They kept talking about how big and unusual it was, just sticking out of the ground like it was. So preoccupied were they, that they forgot that this is supposed to be a talking rock.

"Impressive, huh, boys?" Gramps asked the two chattering boys, who only nodded. "Just wait till you hear it talk."

The two boys instantly fell silent. Once again they glared at each other, this time their eyes were wide open in disbelief. All along they had thought Gramps was teasing them about a talking rock. But now, standing only feet from it, this most trusted of men was again telling them that this rock talks.

"Come see for yourself." He led the boys to a small hole in

the rock, a hole that might be big enough to accommodate a football. "First of all, you want to make sure there's not a skunk in there." Gramps pushed the stick into the hole a few inches and rattled it around. "All clear," he declared. "Now one of you take this stick and hit the rock three times, right there above the hole.

Fossendocker grabbed the stick before Leonard even had his hand out, and gave the rock three solid raps.

"Not so hard!" Boomed a voice from the hole in the rock.

Fossendocker jumped backwards striking Leonard with such force that both boys fell to the ground. They continued to crawl backwards for another five feet.

Gramps could not contain himself, he laughed so hard that tears rolled down his face. The two boys, still on the ground could only glare at him.

"You weren't expecting that, were you?" he finally said. Then Gramps addressed the rock, "Talking rock, I bring two friends."

Again the voice echoed from the hole. "Who are these friends, and which one struck me so hard?"

"Forgive me for failing to instruct my Grandson on how to tap you with the stick. This is Dock and L.L."

"Greetings Dock, greetings L.L."

Leonard managed a very weak, "hello," but Fossendocker wanted no part of talking to a rock. Especially to a rock that would talk back.

The boys finally managed to regain a standing position, while Gramps and the rock conversed about how long it had been since their last visit. Fossendocker, who still had not spoken, was thinking how crazy this all was when the rock said something that really shocked them.

"Joseph, I understand that your wife is making fried pies today. It's been way too long since I've had one of Helena's fried pies."

This was more than Fossendocker could stand. "Gramps,

how can a rock know about Grams' fried pies? How can a rock *eat* a fried pie?" He yelled.

Gramps broke into laughter once again. This time he was joined by the talking rock.

"Come on guys, I'll show you the rest of the rock." Gramps led them around to the opposite side of the big boulder, where much to their surprise, stood Gramps' lifelong friend, Dorsey Raddnick.

The pair of old pranksters shook hands and congratulated each other on a successful prank. It had been many years since they had taken anyone to see the talking rock, and it was obvious that they were thoroughly enjoying themselves.

"Show us how it works," said Leonard. "This is a really good joke. I wish I could get my sister out here."

"See here boys, there's another hole on this side." Mr. Raddnick held a small flashlight just inside the beach ball sized hole. "There is a big hollow space in this rock, you can see the other side and you can see the ceiling, but you can't see the bottom. Listen to this." He dropped a baseball size stone, three seconds later the boys heard a faint splash, as the stone hit water.

"How far down is it to the water, Gramps?" Fossendocker's curiosity was now stirred up.

"We're not really sure," replied Gramps, "we always said we were going to bring a fishing rod and check it, but for some reason we never did."

Fossendocker and Leonard got over the shock of the talking rock pretty soon and laughed along with Gramps and Mr. Raddnick as they recalled stories of the dozens of times they had pulled this same prank on unsuspecting friends.

Finally Gramps suggested that they head home. Mr. Raddnick had taken part of the day off from the hardware store and was going to join Gramps for lunch. Indeed it had been too long since he had enjoyed one of Grams' fried pies.

With full stomachs, Gramps, Mr. Raddnick, and the two

boys retired to the family room. In the meantime Grams, Mrs. Bill, and Raelynn began the fried pies. Soon the whole house was filled with the smells of apples, cinnamon, and chocolate.

Small talk, tales from the good old days, and hearty laughter flowed freely from the two aging gentlemen. The pair of eleven-year-old's were thoroughly entertained. Slapping himself on the knee, Mr. Raddnick proclaimed that they should do this more often. Both boys wholeheartedly agreed to this, but Gramps was quick to point out that everyone would soon tire of their same old stories.

"No one would want to be around us," Gramps continued, "then we would be sitting here like two old goons telling each other the same old stories that we already know about."

"I reckon you're right, Joseph," Mr. Raddnick said. "That would be a sight, wouldn't it?"

"Well, that being the case, maybe you shouldn't come back for a while." Gramps paused, rubbing his chin as if he were in deep thought. "What do you think, Dorse, maybe four or five years. Most likely these young sprouts will have forgotten all these tales by then."

"I reckon you're right again, Joseph. I guess I'll be going." Mr. Raddnick stood and started toward the front door.

"Wait!" yelled Fossendocker. "What about your fried apple pie?"

Both boys were completely caught by surprise. How could he agree not to come back for four or five years and then just leave without a fried pie.

"Yeah, Gramps, don't let him go without a fried pie," added Leonard, equally concerned with the situation.

It was than that Mr. Raddnick turned from the door with a big grin on his face. "We got 'em again Joseph."

Their laughter was interrupted by Grams and Mrs. Bill as they entered the family room each carrying two shallow bowls containing a fried apple pie, a large scoop of vanilla ice cream, and a spoon.

"That should keep you all quiet for awhile," joked Grams as she handed Gramps his bowl. "Dock, Lenny, there's chocolate pies in the kitchen, you two can take those home with you."

Both boys beamed and nodded, but elected not to speak since their mouths were full. Thanks *would* be expressed later, though.

Grams stopped in the doorway to the kitchen and turned to watch her husband of more than forty years as he enjoyed this rare treat. A month shy of his sixty-fifth birthday, he was still a handsome man. Shifting her gaze to her eleven-year-old grandson, she had to smile. How in the world could a boy that looks so different from his grandfather, act so much like him? Looking back at Gramps, their eyes met. He smiled and winked at her before taking another bite of his dessert. Grams felt that certain happiness that only her family could bring welling up inside her. Her eyes moistened a little as that happiness overfilled her heart. She quietly returned to the kitchen and rejoiced.

CHAPTER 13

The next few days flew by. Leonard's parents returned from their vacation and amongst excited chatter and laughter, they told all about their trip. Everyone took turns looking at photos on their digital camera, and shared stories of how beautiful it was in the Rocky Mountains. Then they left, taking their boy with them. They brought him on Sunday after church and they picked him up on Sunday after church.

For the next day and a half Fossendocker hardly left the house. Things just weren't the same. Oh sure, he'd made a new friend in Hut, and he would make more new friends, but in the meantime he sorely missed Leonard.

"Okay, buddy, that's more than enough moping around." Fossendocker's mother gave him a big hug trying to cheer him up. "Today is Tuesday, tomorrow we're going to shop for new school clothes and school supplies while they are on sale. Friday we have to take your transfer papers and get everyone registered at your new schools."

"Oh Mom," he mumbled, "please don't talk about that. I

don't think I'm going to like this new school."

"Sure you will," she tried to sound positive. "But what I'm saying is, for now you should be enjoying your summer vacation because there's only a few days left. Why don't you ride over and visit with Gramps. Grams said he's sitting on the front porch with a big pack of chewing gum just waiting on somebody to come by and help him chew it."

Reluctantly he agreed to go see Gramps. Pretty bad when he doesn't want to go see Gramps, thought Mrs. Bill. I wonder what's up, it seems to be more than just missing Lenny. She watched as her down-trodden little boy peddled his bike down the driveway.

"Be careful on the road," she called out to him then whispered, "maybe Gramps can cheer you up." Then she said a quiet prayer, "please watch over my son, Lord, I never imagined that going to this new school would cause his so much distress."

Gramps was on the front porch all right. He was sitting in his favorite rocking chair with the biggest ball of chewing gum in his mouth that Fossendocker had ever seen. He kept staring at the bulge in his cheek.

"How many pieces of gum do you have in your mouth, Gramps?"

"Seventeen," he casually replied, "would you like some?"

Fossendocker unwrapped a piece of chewing gum. "Gramps, why do you have *seventeen* pieces of gum in your mouth at one time?"

"Way back yonder when I was a boy," he began, "my old Grandpa used to chew tobacco."

"Yuck!" exclaimed Fossendocker. "That's nasty!"

"That was before they figured out that tobacco would rot your teeth out and cause cancer and stuff. But you're right, it was nasty. My Grandpa and some of the other men would have a big wad of that stuff in their jaw, and it would stick out like this." Gramps rubbed the bulge in his cheek. "I always wondered what it

192

would feel like having that much, of something, in your jaw. I'm thankful to the Great Father that I never picked up the bad habit of tobacco in any form. I wouldn't put chewing tobacco in my mouth even if I had some. And I already told you what happened when I tried to chew that rabbit tobacco." Fossendocker chuckled, remembering Gramps' recollection. "I hadn't thought about that in years, till I was watching a baseball game on television last night. There was this young fellow that hit a home run to win the game. He had a great big wad of something in his mouth and when they interviewed him after the game he said that he always has seventeen pieces of gum in his mouth when he's playing. It's his lucky number, and guess what number he wears? Yep, you got it, seventeen. Anyway, that got my curiosity up again and I figured it was high time I find out how a big wad in the jaw felt. So, it came down to a choice between a golf ball and the Halloween goodies your Grams picked up yesterday at the Bargain Bucks. Everything boils down to choices, Dock, remember that. Don't worry, though, it's sugar free." Gramps chuckled and offered more gum to his grandson. "You want to try it? Five or six pieces will probably do you."

"Maybe just one more piece," said Fossendocker, solemnly thanking his grandfather.

The two sat there slowly rocking, chewing their gum, and staring down towards the creek for ten minutes or so before Gramps finally spoke. "What's on your mind, Dock? You sure are quiet today."

"Dub Dillard Junior."

"Oh, I see," answered Gramps. "What about Dub Dillard Junior?"

"He's a lot older that me, and he's flunked three times. Hut says that he's a bully, and he'll pick on me because I'll be the new guy, and because I wear glasses, and because of my name." Then for the next several minutes he spoke freely to his Grandfather about his concerns. "I'm okay with going to a new school, and I know I can make lots of new friends. But nobody wants to be picked on. Nobody wants to be bullied," he added quietly.

Gramps listened intently while rolling his big wad of chewing gum around in his mouth. But now that he was ready to speak, he took it out and placed it on the porch railing. "I'd best not drop this in Grams' flower bed. She might step on it; wouldn't that be a mess?" Gramps leaned back in his rocker, tight lipped, and nodded his head for a few seconds.

"Dock, just because Dub Junior had failed three times, don't make the mistake of assuming that he's not able to learn. The chances are pretty good that he has, at least, average intelligence. But, for some reason his thinking and his actions are going in the wrong direction. I suspect that his choices have been influenced by the choices that his daddy has made. You ever thought about that, Dock? About how your choices might effect the choices other folks make. That's something else to remember. But, I sure hope and pray that he young fellow gets back on track before things really go bad for him." Gramps rose from his rocking chair. "Think about that for a minute while I go get us a glass of iced tea." He retrieved the ball of gum from the porch rail and entered the house.

A few seconds later he smiled as he heard Grams scolding Gramps for chewing so much gum at one time.

"Another thing, Dock," continued Gramps as he reclaimed his rocking chair and handed Fossendocker his glass of tea. "Sometimes folks do things to cover up fears, or pain in their lives. It's like, if they do something to draw attention, or cause somebody else a problem, they won't have to deal with what's really eating at them. I hope you can make some kind of sense out of this. Maybe not now, but maybe after you've had time to think about for a couple of days."

Fossendocker was obviously a little confused, so Gramps tried again.

"Well, let me put it another way." Gramps spoke slowly and deliberately. "Sometimes people that have problems, would rather cause somebody else a problem, than face their own problems."

"I got it, Gramps." Fossendocker nodded. "Now I just need to figure out what to do about it." The older man could see an encouraging glimmer of hope in the boys eyes.

"Good, now let's go down to the barn and see what we can get into. While we're down there I'll have a word with the Great Father on your behalf. That always helps, Dock, try to remember that, too."

Four o'clock came all too quickly and following the instructions of his mother, Fossendocker was on his way back home. Unable to resist, he stopped his bike on the bridge, leaned on the rail and watched the waters of Brightwell Creek flow beneath him. Suddenly, the all too familiar sound of Dub Dillard Junior's dirt bike struck his ears, and in a few seconds he was within sight, carelessly speeding toward the bridge. Instinctively, Fossendocker waved a hello, and much to his surprise Dub slammed on his brakes and pulled to a stop.

"*What*?" Dub asked sharply.

"I'm Fossendocker Bill, I start the sixth grade at Midway Middle School next week and I just—"

"*Fossendocker*!" howled Dub. "That's got to be the stupidest name I've ever heard. I saw you on TV, you and that other looser, the day they were doing that thing for that crazy old woman that makes chicken salad. I laughed at you then, and I'm laughing at you now."

"But I just wanted to intro—"

"Look, dill weed, this is *my* territory, the sixth grade is *my* grade. *I* run the show at that school. Everybody knows that. So, you're mine, shrimp, you got that." With that he fired up his motorbike and was gone in an instant.

A little shook up, Fossendocker boarded his bike and peddled off. "What a jerk," he mumbled as he crossed on over the bridge.

Fossendocker put a lot of thought into the Dub Dillard Junior situation over the next two days and still no solution had come to him. He was quiet certain that introducing Ralph to Dub would make the problem go away, but that's not how he wanted to handle it. This was his problem and he firmly believed that somehow it would work out. But apparently in the mean time he would have to put up with some harassment from the bully.

***

Friday morning, with Raelynn in tow, Mrs. Bill escorted Fossendocker to the offices of Midway Middle School. There they met the principal, Mr. Stone, and Mrs. Timms, the office manager. All the transfer papers were in order and soon the registration process was complete.

"Your homeroom teacher will be Miss Carden," said Mrs. Timms. "She's new here this year, but I'm sure you'll like her." She typed on the computer keyboard for another minute then produced a printed copy of Fossendocker's class schedule. "Miss Carden is in room eighteen, if you would like to go meet her. Just go down to the second hall, turn left, then it's the second room on the right."

The meeting with Miss Carden went very well. She was a pretty lady, about thirty, with sparkling eyes and a gracious smile. Her kind voice put Fossendocker at ease, and he was already feeling much better about this new school.

Much better, that is, until Dub Dillard Junior walked in. Wearing the same cotton plaid shirt with the sleeves cut out that he'd had on three days prior, it looked like it had been at least that long since his last bath and shampoo. The only thing that kept his stringy, greasy-looking hair out of his face was the grungy baseball cap that he wore backwards on his head.

Strolling to the teachers desk he rudely interrupted Mrs. Bill in mid-sentence. "Say you're the new teacher, huh. Well lucky

196

you, I'm in your room. I'm Dub Dillard Junior, my real name is Willard Wayne Dillard, Junior." Dub then leaned over Miss Carden's desk to get closer to her face and said in a very serious voice. *"Don't you ever call me that.* Fix it on your roll sheet. It's *Dub, D U B*, got that, *Dub.*"

Wheeling to leave the room, he stopped to glare at Fossendocker. "Hey, shrimp, you just remember what I told you." He looked up and down Fossendocker's skinny frame, shook his head as if he were disgusted, and then he was gone.

"Who in the world was that obnoxious, nasty smelling, little.....individual?" asked Mrs. Bill, biting her lip to keep from saying what she really wanted to say.

Without hesitation, Fossendocker answered. "That was Willard Wayne Dillard, Junior, but he'd rather be called Dub. He doesn't know it yet, but we are going to be friends."

"What!" exclaimed his mother. She'd instinctively gathered Raelynn closer to her. "Don't be ridiculous, you *do not* need a friend like him!"

"I know, Mom," he replied in a surprisingly calm and serious voice. "I know I don't need a friend like him, but he *does* need a friend like me."

Mrs. Bill was stunned into silence. She searched her mind for what to say next, but there wasn't anything. Her gaze slowly shifted from her son to the new teacher. It was obvious that she too had been moved by the profoundness of the boy's statement.

"Mrs. Bill," said Miss Carden softly, "he may very well be right."

Mrs. Bill smiled solemnly, and replied with a little nod of her head. She then slipped one arm around her son's shoulders, caught Raelynn by the hand, bid the teacher a good day, and led them both into the hallway. They walked silently past the offices and through the front door. Her mind was still processing the words she had heard from her child. They sounded so mature. She had never heard anything come out of Fossendocker's mouth that sounded mature. A part of her was impressed, another part of her was not ready to see her little boy be anything, but a little boy.

Once outside she guided the young ones to a bench near the flagpole and sat down. "Is there anything you would like to tell me about that young fellow we saw in there? Obviously it was not the first time you two have met. Am I right?"

"We met at the bridge the other day," he answered casually, "but there's nothing I want to say about him right now."

"There's *nothing* you want to say?" repeated his mother.

"Well, Mom, maybe. I've been thinking....about my name. I have a really dumb name, and sometimes people make fun of me on account of it. Mom, I don't want to be made fun of."

His mother smiled and squeezed his hand. "I know you don't want to be made fun of. So let me tell you about your name. Your name is far from dumb, and you need not be ashamed, or embarrassed by it. Your name is a worthy name, even more so than all the rest of the family. It was given to you by your grandfather when he somehow knew you would become who you are. Let me explain." She took a deep breath and began. Fossendocker listened intently and even Raelynn was paying attention to her mother's words.

"According to family stories, after our ancestors occupied the swamps for a time, the words of the People began to change. New words were made to fit their needs, and new names as well. Keep in mind that everything was different from their old home. There were different kinds of animals and the landscape was completely different. The People had to learn new ways of building houses. New ways of growing crops, hunting, and gathering food. Your name, Fossendocker, is the English version of the word that came into being to describe a man who could adapt very well to his surroundings in the swamps, find shelter and food, and live without fear. The word 'fossendocker' sounds a little different in the language of the People, and nowadays is most often used to describe one who is in harmony with nature. Watching you grow up, I can see that you have the perfect name for the kind of man you will become."

Fossendocker silently peered up at his mother's face, blinking.

"Maybe I should have told you all of that sooner, but I was worried you wouldn't understand."

"I do understand, Mom, but I'm eleven-years-old now, in middle school, Mom. And I think I would like to be called just plain, Dock."

Mrs. Bill nodded, "I think we can manage that."

"Thanks Mom," Dock jumped to his feet and hugged his mom tightly around the neck. "In harmony with nature, huh, that's pretty cool." He then started for the car.

"Foss.....I mean, Dock, wait, there's something else." The boy returned to the bench. "Being in harmony with nature is pretty cool, but there is One that is much greater than all of nature, and it is much more important to be in harmony with Him. The Great Father, as Gramps calls Him. God, our Heavenly Father, our Savior, as others call Him." Mrs. Bill reached for Dock's hand. "And from the way you've cast your eyes downward at the mention of His name, it causes me to believe that you have felt His calling."

***

Dock was very quiet for the remainder of the day, as well as Saturday. He avoided making eye contact with either of his parents, and stayed out of sight as much as possible. He even turned down an offer from his mom to go with her to see Gramps and Grams. Much to the concern of his parents, he spent long periods in deep thought.

When night finally came he put himself to bed much earlier than usual. His heart pounded. He had indeed felt God's call.

The following morning Dock sat in silence on the way to

church. He hardly spoke to Lenny during Sunday School, and then claimed a seat between his parents for the service. Something he hadn't done in years. Mr. and Mrs. Bill looked at one another with understanding and compassion for their son. They were not at all surprised when the invitation was given and Dock stepped into the aisle, and made his way to the alter.

Dock really didn't know how to pray. He really didn't know how to invite Jesus into his heart, but he did know that was what he wanted. So for several minutes he listened to his pounding heart, then he became aware that there were others knelt around him. He could hear prayers being offered up on his behalf. He recognized those voices. He heard his mom's voice, and his dad's. Then there was Lenny's mom, and Gramps and Grams. All praying for him. Suddenly some of his misbehavior flashed before him; not everything he'd ever done, some were thoughtless, silly things that most kids do. Other transgressions, however, were not so innocent: Not admitting to breaking Mrs. Hambee's flower pot. Turning Mr. Garrett's trash can over, and then laughing for a week about the half-hour rage he unleashed on his neighbor, as he falsely accused his neighbors German Shepard of the crime. The rotten things he had planned to do with Ralph's love-letter that he'd found. Provoking Rhonda to the point of using foul language with that telephone prank. The list, seemingly, went on and on, and with a broken heart Dock asked for forgiveness. He didn't want to be an unruly troublemaker, he wanted to be a decent person, honor God, and be the benefactor of His many blessings.

And then God's peace blanketed the boy. His broken heart was mended, forgiveness chased away his guilt, and he knew he was forever changed. Dock immediately stood and with a beaming face announced to the pastor, "I am now a Child of God."

The church members rejoiced and celebrated with hugs and handshakes. When Gramps hugged him, Dock proudly proclaimed, "the Great Father lives in my heart."

Gramps held him at arms length, smiled, and replied, "as

well as mine, my Grandson."

Dock was almost as quiet on the ride home from church as he had been that morning, but for a different reason. Now he savored being in harmony with the Great Father. He felt lighthearted and he was thankful.

The Bill family was on their way to Gramps' and Grams' house to grill hamburgers, so they bypassed their own driveway and continued toward Brightwell Creek. As they neared the bridge, though, Dock had a strange feeling in his chest. "Dad, will you please stop at the bridge?" Mr. Bill stopped the SUV just short of the bridge and turned to gaze inquisitively at his son.

"Is it okay if I walk the rest of the way?" He saw his mom reach over and place her hand on his dad's forearm and give him a slight nod. He, in turn, nodded at Dock, but did not speak.

Dock watched as the car went around the curve and out of sight before he walked onto the bridge. He stopped and gazed at the water flowing below him. Dub Dillard Junior was heavy on his mind. The incident on the bridge flashed into his memory, when Dub Dillard Junior had treated him so rudely. Only now, he no longer felt intimidated, and he felt no anger towards the strange young fellow. The insightful words of his grandfather rang clearly in his mind and he, too, was concerned for the wayward boy. Maybe this is what people at church call a burden, he thought. Maybe I have a burden for Dub. Continuing to watch the water below, he whispered a prayer. "Great Father, I am new at this, but somehow I will be a friend to Dub Dillard Junior, and somehow I will let him know about You."

Dock started on towards his grandparents' house, happily whistling the four note bird call Gramps had taught him, as he went. He was still the same mischievous, fun-loving boy that he'd always been, and always would be, but now he *was* different. Just *how* different would surprise everyone, but the one most surprised would be Fossendocker Bill.

BILL DALE GRIZZLE

202

Available on Amazon
or
signed copies may be ordered directly at
billdalegrizzle@aol.com

also, look for
Mandy the Mischievous Elf
and
Mandy the Mischievous Elf: Mandy's Triplets
(coming before Christmas 2019)

BILL DALE GRIZZLE

Made in the
USA
Columbia, SC

81973310R00114